TRIXTER

Alethea Kontis

The Trix Adventures Book One
Books of Arilland Volume 2.5

TRIXTER
The Trix Adventures Book One
Books of Arilland, Volume 2.5
© 2015 by Alethea Kontis

www.aletheakontis.com

Cover Design by Rachel Marks
Interior Design by Polgarus Studio

Books of Arilland

Enchanted

Hero

Trixter

Dearest

(Messenger)

Thieftess

Fated

Endless

Countenance

*

Tales of Arilland

Other Titles by Alethea Kontis

Beauty & Dynamite

Wild & Wishful, Dark & Dreaming

The Dark-Hunter Companion (w / Sherrilyn Kenyon)

AlphaOops: The Day Z Went First

AlphaOops: H is for Halloween

The Wonderland Alphabet

Elemental (editor)

For Josh and Madoc,
Whose adventures continue in a world beyond this one.

1

The Boy Who Talks to Animals

rix Woodcutter ignored the twinges in his belly and the ache in his heart as he raced across the meadow. It hadn't been the most graceful of escapes. If he'd had more time to plan, he would have arranged to meet a deer-friend or one of the lynx outside the towerhouse so that he might have covered more ground before the dark magic brew in his system took effect. A deer might have been the better choice as he was (finally) getting too tall to ride a lynx comfortably. If he'd really been clever, then—

PAIN.

Trix gasped. Winced. Doubled over. Cramps stabbed through his middle like knives and he cried out despite himself. He'd had bad porridge before, but this was beyond anything he'd ever experienced. His hands balled into fists and instinctively tried to reach for the tiny army with pointy swords fighting a battle to the death inside him so that he could *make it all stop*.

He tripped. Rolled. Paused, waiting for the—

—PAIN—

—to pass so that he could keep moving. He took a deep breath. The razor sharp flashes of anger inside him subsided enough to let him back up. He shuffled, walked, ran—*PAIN*—shuffled, jogged, all while trying to think about something besides the incredibly stupid decision he'd just made.

It would have been impossible to successfully bespell his family without bespelling himself, even just a little. It was all Mama's fault; Mama, with those eagle eyes of hers that saw everything and the silver tongue that could make the devil do her bidding. Being raised by a woman whose every statement came true had taught him to always seek forgiveness instead of permission. His quest was too important this time. One "no" from Mama's lips would have stopped Trix from leaving the house entirely. So he had put her to sleep—put them all to sleep—to avoid her saying anything at all.

Eagles. The cleverest thing to do would have been to call the eagles and *really* fly, though they would have disapproved of him betraying his family. Eagles were all about loyalty. An eagle would never have crossed his congregation. Trix wasn't particularly proud of himself either, at the moment. He deserved whatever horrible pain he was in.

He cried out and doubled over again. He checked to see if he'd split in two without realizing it, but he spotted no blood on his tunic. He coughed through a particularly wrenching spasm—no blood there either. That last fall had torn his trousers, though. Trix laughed a little as he pulled himself to standing and shuffled forward a few more drunken steps. He told himself that a magicked stomach ache was surely preferable to the whipping Mama would give him if she caught him.

Trix screamed. The cramps wracked his whole body this time, bringing tears to his eyes.

"Maybe the whippings weren't so bad after all," he said to no one. At least he'd known when those would end.

One more step. Two. Three. Three more steps. It was going to take him days to cross this meadow. Years. A lifetime. He deserved it, too, every moment of crippling agony, every scrape, every tear. Family didn't do this to each other. And yet…

Three days ago, he never would have put a sleeping spell on the stew and poisoned his sister, his brother, the man and woman who had raised him from a babe and never treated him like anything but their own. Three days ago, it never would have crossed his mind to do such a selfish and horrible thing. But three days ago his birthmother hadn't appeared in his dreams and called for him.

Earth breaks; fire breathes; waters bless. Fly to me, my son.

Trix knew what dreams looked like, the real dreams, the ones he was meant to pay attention to. They had more in them than the nothing-dreams of restless nights: more color, more feel, more sound, more taste, more cohesiveness, more details, more memory than memory. Real dreams did not fade upon waking but instead became more vivid, replaying themselves over and over in the mind's eye until the brain teetered on madness with the vision. Real dreams came from the gods. The gods knew how to make a point.

The gods also knew how to abandon someone in their time of need.

Trix would never have been able to convey the urgency of those dreams. The journey to Rose Abbey was one he needed to make immediately and alone. There was also a very good chance that the spell he'd put on the stew wouldn't work. It's not as if he had tried such a thing before—

PAIN.

Oh, the spell had definitely worked. Perhaps a little too well. Shame, too, because that stew had smelled delicious—one of his better accidental concoctions.

"It would have been nice to leave on a full stomach," he said, before recalling that no one was around to hear him.

Between the Woodcutter family and his animal friends, Trix was never alone in the world. And yet tonight there did not seem to be a soul within sight. Trix heard barely a cricket chirp above his ragged breathing. The twilight he escaped into offered a rare solitude. It was at the same time peaceful and concerning.

A silent Wood, in the main, usually meant trouble.

Trix stumbled again, forced himself back to standing and stayed there for a moment, listening. The wind had picked up.

Trix glanced over his shoulder—he could still make out the very top of the Woodcutter home just above the whipping, writhing grasses of the meadow. Dark clouds gathered in the west, swallowing the sun, but not before something in the tower window caught the fading light and flashed it back at him, like a lighthouse beacon on a foreign shore.

Like a warning.

The world fell completely silent then, as if Trix had stopped his ears with beeswax. The leaves were silent, his breath was silent, his heartbeat was silent. Even the wind was silent.

A moment later, the silence transformed into ceaseless thunder: first a low grumble, and then a growl as the earth bucked and reared, furious and alive.

The ground fell away before him. Trix came down hard on his knees. The meadow rolled beneath his feet, bending and waving like a sea of tall grass…on a sea of tall grass. He was caught up in the fray, helpless to regain his footing, so he tried to ride the earth as it slid and slipped beneath him.

He failed spectacularly.

In addition to the grass and dirt now slamming into his face, Trix could sense magic on the wind. Old magic. It was the smell of stag and the Elder Wood, of loam rich with time. He tasted it, sharp and stingful, mixed with dust and rain. The skies roared and the ground answered. Water plummeted from the sky. The patch of meadow beneath his feet split and bled dark, earthy blood.

Trix realized now that the gods had not seen to his needs because they were obviously busy doing something else. And, he also realized, he *should* have been worrying. Or praying. Or apologizing. Or *something*.

"Benevolent gods," he managed to squeak into the din. "I implore—"

The crack beneath him split further apart. The earth bucked, throwing him forward. He bit his tongue, catching himself unevenly on another green and brown wave of tumbling rocks and roots. He tasted blood as his face met the ground, over and over. Somewhere in his body he felt at least one bone crack, but he couldn't tell *where*, what with the earth still roiling and pummeling him unceasingly.

He was not a sailor and had no sense of sea, be it composed of waves of water or dust. The tossing finally got the best of him, and his wretched stomach emptied itself of what little of the poisoned stew Trix had consumed at the dinner table.

He should have felt better. He did not. Nothing would be "better" until the ground stopped moving. The torrential rain did not wash his face clean so much as muddy it further, making it even more difficult to breathe. He closed his eyes and mouth to spare them the influx of dirt, but he was forced to open them again when he reached out to lever himself off the ground and his hand met nothing.

The shifting meadow had tossed him directly onto another, larger crack, one that trembled beneath his belly. His clothes grew increasingly damp with mud and rain and blood and tears and vomit. Trix was distracted from standing, however, not by the shuddering landscape, but by the spider he noticed painstakingly making her way through what was left of the meadow grasses.

She carried a spun sack on her back.

The crack beneath him split in to two, and then two more. He quickly realized that neither side of the small crevasse that currently bisected his body was the "wrong" side; he just needed to choose one. The only wrong decision would be not making one. And so he chose.

Trix swept the spider carefully up into his hands and rolled...and rolled...and did not stop.

The earth pushed Trix along. It cracked and shifted beneath him, bubbling with hot mud and the smell of burnt foliage and old magic. Trix curled his body into a ball as the mud burned his— arm, yes, his left forearm had sustained one of those breaks. Between that pain and the beating the rest of his body was receiving as the quake tossed him about, he could barely discern the stomach cramps anymore.

Trix had always been a fan of small favors.

He protected his tiny ward as best he could and attempted to coax their wild ride into some sort of planned direction...but to what end? As far as he knew, the Wood was tilting as wildly as the meadowland. Unless he grew wings in the next few breaths and removed himself completely from the pull of the Earth Goddess, there would be no surcease from the constant motion.

Trix banged his head on a rock, or the rock banged into him...regardless, he tucked into himself as much as he could and addressed his passenger in the small hollow his body created.

"Hullo there." Trix tried to keep his voice level. He'd learned the hard way in the Wood that when one encountered a mother with small children, one took great care to remain calm. He hoped she wasn't able to smell the sick on his breath.

"Hello, Boy Who Talks to Animals and Stealer of Spiders."

"Apologies for the kidnapping, madam," Trix said politely. "My name is Trix." The last bit of name was lost along with his wind as a particularly sharp rock encountered his right side. If he didn't have a broken rib before, he certainly had one now.

"I'm Needa, and these are my children," she said. "Bless you for the ride."

"Don't bless me yet. It's not over, and I'm considerably worse for the wear." As if she couldn't tell from the bumps and jolts that brought him to within a hairsbreadth of squashing her every time. He grunted as they were unceremoniously thrown what seemed like a considerable distance, and then pelted with clods of dirt. The gods were surely busy at the moment, but he sent out a futile prayer regardless. He wanted to remain in one piece, if only for the sake of his passenger.

Then again, it was possible that one of the gods had his or her eye on Trix. It did seem a miracle that he could sustain an actual conversation amidst such chaos. The spider, too, might have been responsible for that...spiders were known for having all sorts of mischief-magic, the nature of which was shrouded in mystery. It was a facet of arachnids Trix had always admired.

"Might you have any idea what's going on?" he asked Needa.

"The animals of the Wood sensed the Fear," she said. "I should have run with them, but I could not leave my children. By the time I was ready to catch a gust, the wind was too wild. It kept dashing me into the ground."

"The Fear?" asked Trix. He was fluent enough in animal-speak that he could sometimes communicate on a transcendent level, but he'd had no notion of this Fear of which she spoke. "What does it feel like?"

"It is a knowing," said Needa. "The Fear pulls deep in your belly and forces your feet to run. You know that you must go, and so you go."

Trix had not noticed anything like this pull; perhaps his belly had been too preoccupied with all the lovely stabbing reminders of his idiocy. "You run, even if you don't know why?"

"There is always a why," said Needa. "It just doesn't matter. Saving oneself matters. And one's family."

Even so indisposed, Trix was surprised not to have any inkling of this. "I did not sense this Fear."

"You are too fey, Boy Who Talks to Animals. It has masked the animal in you."

Needa's scolding reminded him of Mama, with her hands on her hips and flour in her hair. Trix wasn't aware that he had any animal inside him in the first place, so he felt honored at this discovery. "Not that it matters, but do you happen to know the why? Why this is—*oof*—happening?"

"A goddess wakes," Needa said in her small voice, "a very unhappy goddess."

"That does explain things." Trix set about trying to balance himself on his rump as the ground beneath him liquefied. He kept the spider cradled in his broken arm and used his legs as rudders in the shifting sea of mud. It was much like sledding down the hills in winter, only without a sled. Or snow. Warm mud filled his shoes and trousers. Sharp sticks and stones tore at his shirt and bit into his palms.

"Would you be so kind as to throw us to the wind, Boy Who Talks to Animals?"

It seemed a risky suggestion. "What if you are dashed to the ground again?"

"I'll take my chances," said Needa. "I suspect I may be swept away at any moment as it is."

"All right," said Trix. "I'm going to set you in my hair while I tame this wild beast. You just hold on."

He placed the spider gently in the hair above his forehead. There was a large boulder bobbing up and down in the sea of mud to his right. If he could just make it over there… The muscles in his legs screamed for mercy. He forced them to obey him just a little bit longer.

Trix had actively, brilliantly avoided responsibility for most things in his life. This situation left him no wild warren to escape to, with no animal friend to assist him and no sibling who could solve the problem smarter or better or faster. This time, survival was all up to him and it was *important*. Enthusiastic carelessness was not an option. The thought that so much depended on him was frightening. And not in the same way as Needa's Fear: that seemed to be an instinct that told a body to run. The terror Trix felt right now came with the duty to stay.

Before he knew it, the boulder was upon them, or they were upon it, and with a sort of belch and squelch, the earth spat Trix and Needa on top of it. Not that being on the rock was much better than surfing the mud itself…

Trix immediately flipped onto his stomach, found rough crevasses in which to shove his strong hand and feet, and held on for dear life. Fire and fright took turns washing through his body; Trix concentrated on staying conscious.

They spun and tipped, but thankfully did not roll over. Trix tried to use his meager body weight to keep his strange ship from capsizing. He imagined it worked, but then, he could imagine a lot of things. For instance, he could imagine that the cries of terror issuing from his forelock were actually shrieks of joy as the rock bucked and twisted. The wind, too, seemed to finally have direction…but which direction, he knew not. The unhappy goddess had confused that as well. What was once up was now down, and contrariwise.

When he felt that he had enough control, he called out to Needa, "Are you ready to fly?"

"No time like the present," he heard her say. He reached up with his good arm and cupped his hand as gently as he could over his hair until he felt her many feet tickle his palm. Trix held the tiny spider in his trembling hand—trembling not from fear, but as the rock beneath them trembled. He waited while Needa secured her egg sacks to her back once again.

"I did not get to know you," said the spider, "and we will not meet again, but I would thank you, Boy Who Talks to Animals. I will tell the King of Spiders of your selflessness."

"Live for me," Trix told her. "Let your children live. That will be thanks enough."

"Fare well, my friend," said the spider.

"I shall try," Trix replied.

"Oh, you will," said the spider. But whether she meant that he would fare well or that he would try, Trix had no time to clarify. With agile legs the spider cast her net wide. The gossamer silk immediately caught the gusting wind. Dark spouts of wind and earth and water stretched up from the ground to the clouds as she passed, like giant hands of hungry demons trying to catch her.

Trix lay there on the tilting rock looking after the spot in the sky where Needa and her eggs had vanished, sending prayers for her safe travels into the sky. He was still praying when the sea swallowed him whole.

2

The Custom of Falling Stars

he rock he had been using as a platform quickly
became an anchor. Trix let go and gave himself to the
maelstrom. Over and over he tumbled through the waves, above
and below. Darkness and light flashed before him. Darkness meant
water. Light meant air. Trix concentrated, attempting to breathe
only into the light. Even still, every time he opened his mouth,
what entered was half water. At first, it tasted of murky rain
puddles. Then it became briny, like tears.

The sea.

Somehow, the sea was coming inland.

A tiny part of Trix—the part that wasn't desperate to survive—
was overjoyed. He'd never seen the ocean before. Apparently his
visit to the seaside was so long overdue that the impatient ocean

had packed its bags and come to see Trix instead. How polite the ocean was! Very big and scary, of course, but very kind. Assuming it didn't kill him in the process…which suddenly seemed a distinct possibility.

Another part of Trix—the part that was concerned about the seawater now flooding into his mouth—was sad at the thought that he might never speak again. Not to the animals who were his friends; not to the family who would still love him despite his terrible behavior. Trix had to leave them for this quest, but he'd always planned to return. Shameful that his last act had not been one of love, but tricks and tales. The thought of never seeing Mama and Papa and Peter and all his sisters again added to the shame in his heart, the pain in his broken limbs, and the ache in his chest for want of a lungful of good air.

As he spun wildly in the churning tumult, randomly alternating betwixt air-not-water and water-not-air, he was reminded of something an old river trout had told him. When there was rain, or a terrible storm, or even rowdy children cavorting about on a summer's day, the water was only disturbed on the surface. To maintain his desired level of peace and quiet, the trout simply swam to deeper depths. Unfortunately, amidst the mayhem, Trix could not discern up from down long enough to choose a safe direction in which to dive.

A large body crashed into him—a bear? A whale?—pushing Trix downward, further into the sea, and those parts of Trix that weren't in terrible pain mentally thanked the stranger for obliging. He opened his eyes—the salty water stung a bit—and tried to quell the fear inside him long enough to get his bearings. The small breath he'd managed to capture in his lungs wouldn't last for long.

He'd not been the only one caught up in this storm. Denizens of earth and sea tumbled above him in terror and confusion. A donkey sped by. A school of purple fish. A wagon full of crabs. A cow, turning leisurely end over end, the bell around her neck silenced.

Trix was a mischief-maker of the first order, but this madness was spectacular.

A turtle sped by and Trix stretched out his good arm, reaching for its foot, but he missed as it pulled back into its protective shell. Something else, a small body, rough and pliant slapped into his palm instead. Trix could not see what it was—it might have been a bundle of wet cloth for all he knew—but it did not matter. He pulled the thing in to him, tucking it inside his shirt. Happily, it was not a bundle of cloth after all; he felt the body stretch out against his chest and hold on to his skin with some sort of knobby tube feet. Trix was no match for this violent sea, but perhaps, with a little luck, he could save this one life.

He wished he could save them all.

Mouth closed and muscles locked, Trix concentrated on the pressure building inside him. The broken ribs felt like shattered glass in his lungs. That one small breath he'd stolen needed to leave him now, and he had to let it go. Trix wondered in that moment about Lord Death and his Angels of Feathers and Fire. Every young child speculated which of the Angels might come for him should he not clean his room or eat his peas, but what Angel delivered those lost at sea into Death's loving embrace? Water was anathema to both feathers *and* fire. It was conceivable that Lord Death also employed Angels of Fins, only no one who saw them ever survived to tell the tale. Maybe it would be Jack Junior or Tuesday, those beloved siblings who had died before him that would appear to usher Trix to the Great Beyond. That would be a small comfort.

Or Death might send Trix's mother to fetch his departed soul. Memory brought her words from his vision back unbidden.

Come to me, my sweetheart. My sweetheart, come to me. There is so much you should know, and still yet so far to go.

Violently and uncontrollably, that small, precious breath he'd been holding escaped him. A murmuration of tiny bubbles fled upward, taunting him with the life he would never get back.

This was it, then. He was going to die. Trix tried to remain calm about it, hoping that his fear would pass from discomfort into acceptance. His body had other plans. It wanted to fight this losing battle. Trix's arms and legs spasmed. He opened his mouth and awaited the unwelcome rush of water that would put an end to his very interesting boyhood.

That end did not come.

Trix took a deep breath of not-air-not-water-but-still-life. Somehow he continued to live, suspended in this watery otherworld.

He felt a humming vibration from the tubed feet on his chest. Reaching into his shirt, he traced the body of the animal there. It felt a bit like the tail of a large lizard...but a lizard with five tails and no body. The vibration emanated from the center of the animal, resonating through Trix from the top of his head to the tips of his toes. It was a comfortable, tingly feeling—pleasant even in the broken places. The vibration washed his pain away, as well as the chill of the increasingly frigid waters.

And then the hum turned to words—not in Trix's ears, but in that place in his mind where he heard things. *I'm scared*, said the hum.

So am I, Trix hum-thought in return.

The tube feet squirmed on Trix's skin. It might have been a reaction of surprise or happiness—whatever it was, accompanied by the tingling vibration it tickled mightily. Trix's body twitched involuntarily in response. The muscles of the animal contracted and gripped Trix's chest like the fingers of a strong man, a man keen on ripping Trix's heart clean out of his chest.

Hello, Boy Who Talks to Animals.

Trix grinned into the not-air. He and his sisters often spoke to each other without words, but never like this. He knew such a thing was possible but he'd always assumed it was a talent reserved only for animal-kind, or the true fey.

Trix answered as calmly as he could manage, with the animalest part of his soul. *Hello!* he said, and almost at the same time, *What are you?*

I am a sea star, said the sea star.

I have never been to the sea, said Trix.

You cannot say that anymore, said the sea star.

Trix smiled at that, the seawater slipping across his teeth as he did so. The salt didn't sting his eyeballs so much anymore. He took advantage of the opportunity to discover what wonders the ocean had dredged up from its depths and brought for him.

Before him played a tumultuous masterpiece.

A melee of brilliant colors swirled above and below him. As the waters rose the larger aquatic life made their way to the bottom, away from the crashing, churning waves far above. Trix grabbed the tail of a large flat beast whose body was also its wings and caught a ride farther down. He realized as they swam that he was holding on with his left hand, the hand connected to the arm that had— until a short while ago—been broken. Perhaps the magic that had summoned this water somehow healed him as well. If that were so, he was a lucky boy indeed.

Schools of shimmering fish slipped by boulders and trees that slammed their way past. Some of the larger beasts were not so lucky. Trix hovered above a kraken who took a chunk of stray chimney in the side, and the watery world in which he floated turned briefly black with ink. Curious, Trix darted the tip of his tongue into the spreading dark cloud. The ink was thinner than blood, bitter and fishy and mysterious. It was all so beautiful to him, this new and strange forest. And it was peaceful here; Trix's mind rarely found such peace. If Death's Angels were coming for him today, he rather hoped they took their sweet time. He was enjoying himself.

Some creatures of the forest were not faring so well. A family of opossums sank slowly as they clung to each other for safety. A herd of confused deer galloped nowhere together, their eyes wild as their legs tread the water below them. From Trix's vantage point it looked as if they were flying above the rooftops below—for there were houses below them now, and barns, and fences, and empty roads traveled by no living soul.

But there were living souls in the sea, Trix realized suddenly. They were—all of them: dogs, cats, fawns and fish alike—still living. He placed his hand over the sea star that still sought asylum on his chest. Beneath the star, Trix's heart was definitely still beating.

How is this possible? Trix asked in his mind.

It is the custom of falling stars to grant a wish, the sea star hummed in return. *Thusly have I granted yours.*

Had he made a wish? Trix remembered only salt and storm and funnel clouds and the songs of impending Angels. *Am I dead?* he asked, though he didn't really want the answer. It was entirely possible that he had subconsciously wished to save his own life, but at what price? There was always a price.

You are not dead, said the star. *Nor is any soul touched by these magical waters. You have saved them, Boy Who Talks to Animals. You have saved us all.*

Trix vaguely recalled such a thought crossing his mind as he had reached for the turtle…and caught the star. He was one very lucky boy indeed. With one exceptionally powerful ally.

I thank you for granting that wish, friend, said Trix. *You did not have to save my life.*

Nor were you obligated to save mine, said the star. *Perhaps we are more alike than one might think.*

I believe you might be right, Trix agreed. *Still, that must have taken a monstrous amount of magic.*

It did, admitted the star. *But it will last. However, I cannot tell you how many of these earth creatures will remember their adventure, once they reach solid ground again.*

Probably for the best, said Trix.

Nor do I know how long you will stay alert, said the star, *so it's best if you tell me now which shore you ultimately wish to alight upon.*

So that was the price to be paid for this magic—he would not get to experience the fullness of his undersea adventure. Shame. He had rather hoped to see a narwhal. Or a capricorn. Or that waking goddess Needa had mentioned; perhaps she only needed someone to talk with to make her less angry. Trix had enough experience with his seven sisters to know.

Despite all that, Trix thought a sleep-spell a fair price indeed. Hadn't he just forced his family to the same fate? *North and east,* he said to the star. *More north than east.*

Noted. We should advance in the direction of… The vibration spread through Trix's limbs again and the sea star's hum changed in tone. *Oh, dear.*

Trix cupped his hands and waved his arms to the left, awkwardly turning in the thick, watery depths. By now, it was clear that the sea star needed no eyes to intuit its surroundings, but Trix had no such talents that he knew of. The shadow of another great beast swam in slow circles above them; the sky was so far away now that Trix had to squint into the darkness. An errant ray of light struck a school of silver fish that darted like a cloud of lightning before him, and then parted to reveal three white shapes before him.

People! Trix thought. *How wonderful!* Magic and adventures were always better when shared.

Not people, hummed the sea star.

Trix was inclined to disagree with his new friend, but he kept his mouth—mind?—shut for the time being. The current created by the beast's passing brought them closer to the almost glowing creatures, close enough for Trix to make out arms and faces. Women! Three women, in fact, barely moving, their skin so sallow that they appeared... Trix made out deep, empty gashes along their rib cages.

This must have been what the sea star meant by "not people"— the women were corpses. Trix had been assured that his wish had saved every living thing in this sea, so these poor, unfortunate souls must have passed away before the magical tide had come rushing in. No doubt the victims of some ghastly murder, buried in a shallow grave, revealed and swept away with the sinks and pots and butter churns. For a moment he saw his sisters in their faces— Friday, Saturday, Sunday—lifeless and just out of reach. The current drew him in closer. He did not pull away.

Their long hair tangled about their limbs, all of it streaked so bright red with blood that Trix could not make out which tresses belonged to whom. Mercifully, some dark cloak still sheathed their lower limbs, and their eyes remained closed. Would some kind person bury this sad trio on a foreign shore, he wondered, or would they ultimately be swept back out to the larger sea?

We should move on, urged the sea star.

Trix felt terrible about abandoning the dead women, but even Mama would have told him there was nothing more to be done here. He began offering up a silent prayer to the Earth Goddess before deciding she probably had her hands full at the moment. Instead, Trix beseeched kindness from Lord Death on behalf of these nameless women and wished them a safe journey in the arms of…whatever Angel came to fetch them. Trix quickly looked about on the off chance he managed to catch a glimpse of his imagined Angel of Fins.

When he looked back, one of the women was staring at him.

One by one, eyelids began to open. Layers of eyelids. The first revealed the milky eyes of the dead. The second revealed the hollow black eyes of monsters. Trix had been wrong. There were no souls in these not-women at all.

RUN! Trix thought-cried.

SWIM! hummed the sea star.

Trix kicked frantically in the water, but his meager legs were no match for the sirens' thick ebony tails, slicing through the current like poisoned daggers. They surrounded him in but an instant, transforming into a violent cloud of translucent white skin and red hair and sharp teeth and those empty, hungry eyes. They reached for him with their bony fingers, colorless but for a splash of crimson at the tip of each one. They snapped at him, snapped at each other as they fought over him.

The great shadow passed above them again, showering the attack in mottled darkness. Trix reached into his shirt and pulled the reluctant sea star from his chest. He could feel the star's hum of fear, but there was no time to explain. *I just hope that's what I think it is.* With all the might he could summon, Trix tossed the star skyward.

He continued to fight off the sirens with everything he had, but they were too fast for him. He felt a hand on his wrist and a mouth on his neck just as the water around them turned black with ink.

Trix took advantage of the sirens' blind confusion and kicked up with all his might, in the same direction he'd thrown the star. As he cleared the ink he realized the retreating shadow was not an octopus, as he'd supposed, but another large animal with similar legendary properties.

A hand gripped Trix's wrist and he flailed about wildly, but it was not bony fingers attached to a siren. He recognized soon enough the feel of familiar knobby feet. *A great squid*, hummed the sea star. *Well done, friend.*

I still cannot swim fast enough, said Trix. The muscles of his poor legs were beyond exhausted. *We cannot escape them.*

We don't need to, said the sea star. *I have called a friend.*

Trix felt another vibration, from outside his skin this time, coming to him through the water itself. Approaching them was the largest turtle Trix had ever seen…but this turtle had no shell, only spotted, leathery skin, and its forelegs were more like flippers than feet. Trix maneuvered himself astride its back and settled his legs into the ridges there. He relaxed slightly as the turtle quickly put more distance between them and the ink cloud of sirens. The energy of all the excitement beginning to leave him. Yes, this would be a good, safe way to travel, for as far as the turtle was willing to take them.

Thank you again, brother-kin, Trix told the sea star.

The address seemed to please the star, whose tube feet wriggled and tickled Trix's skin again. *It is my honor, Boy Who Talks to Animals.*

Excellent. Now then, I may be unconscious soon. Trix's eyelids were already starting to feel the heaviness of sleep-fog. *What other sorts of mischief can we get up to in the meantime?*

The sea star's hum was melodiously pleasurable. *I look forward to telling the King of Stars of this day, and our adventures here.*

So do I, brother-kin, said Trix. *So do I.*

3

The Head of Wisdom

 ome to me, my sweetheart.
My sweetheart, come to me.
There is so much you should know,
And still yet so far to go.

Trix forced his reluctant eyelids open. The world was a russet-stained muddle around him, and from that haze walked the shining image of a woman in a flowing violet dress woven with vines. Her wild cinnamon hair curled around the shafts of light delivered by the morning sun. She bent down and tutted over his barely conscious form but did not touch him.

"It should have been Snow White, you know. Fate dealt my sister all the winning cards, and yet somehow the Faerie Queen still managed to trump her hand. And so I had a son."

His birthmother wore a different costume than she had on previous visits, but she carried herself the same, commanding in both voice and bearing. "Four" she had been born, fourth daughter of his unimaginative grandmother. Until this spring she had been nothing to Trix but a shadowy character in the stories Papa told about his wife's family. Mama never told stories.

"The prophecies of gods must be fulfilled by someone, and I was their backup plan: ill-equipped, untrained, and unprepared. What a disappointment I must be to you. Not that it makes you any less powerful."

Tesera was the name she gave herself before taking the stage and treading boards across the world, returning only to abandon her babe on the doorstep of her fertile little sister so that she could return to her life unburdened.

"I could not know you until now, but I could not be prouder of you, Trix Woodcutter," she said. "You have already accomplished so many wonderful things in your short life. Just think of all the places you have yet to visit, all the adventures you have left to live."

He wanted to speak at her words, but his wretched body would not obey him. There were still secrets left to reveal, questions yet unanswered. Who was his father? Why had she and he *both* abandoned him? What did the gods have planned for him beyond the towerhouse where he grew up? And what in Heaven or Earth was so important that his birthmother's spirit was moved to place a compulsion upon him from the land of the Dead? What weird knowledge did Tesera Mouton have to impart to *him*, a boy she barely knew?

"Fly to me soon, my sweetheart, my son," his mother whispered in his ear. "Earth breaks; fire breathes; waters bless. Both the witch and your father are searching for you. Help us."

Trix owed Tesera Mouton nothing. Help her? He had helped his sister Sunday in her lessons once, guiding her without telling her the answers, and when she had chosen to run from the prince who was her destiny, Trix had run with her. Sunday had always loved Trix, truly and unconditionally. Sunday would have urged him to journey onward, heedless of this nagging vision, and never look back.

Oh, Sunday, how I miss you.

Trix added his tears to the already salty ground. The sobs shot painfully through his aching chest, suppressed for so long and now filling with brilliant burning air that brought with it the briny taste of regret.

"He's taking forever," said a voice.

"Don't be a toad," said a second voice that sounded uncannily similar to the first. "Let the boy have his cry. He's been through a lot, poor minnow. He needs a hug."

"You don't have hands, nitwit," said the toad.

"At least I have a heart," said the nitwit.

"Look, he wasn't the only one tossed about in that mad ocean. We've all been through a lot today."

"It won't kill you to wait a while longer," said the nitwit.

"One of us is already dead. We need his help. You there," called the toad. "Boy! If you're all done with that cry, could you help us out?"

"You could at least say 'please,'" the nitwit said softly.

Trix pushed himself up, though the muscles of his arms had intense feelings about being so tirelessly abused. His shirt was in tatters but his wounds seemed to have healed decently enough. The old blood had washed away in the sea, but an ache in his bones remained. Like when Grinny Tram predicted rain. Well, there *had* been rain. Rather a lot of rain. But Grinny's aches usually came before the storms, not after. Perhaps Trix's aches would reach synchronicity when he was older.

He fell more than turned over and willed his battered body into a sitting position. This was a strange shore. Not strange in the way that he did not recognize it, even though he did not, but strange in that it should have been an old hayfield gone to seed and not the edge of an ocean. The tide had gone out, he surmised, or the waking goddess had spent her anger and collapsed into a fitful sleep.

Beyond the field stretched a horizon of unbroken sea, the crashing waves winking the reflection of the rising sun over and over and over again in a soothing lullaby. Beside him lay a very long, very purple dragon with three heads.

"Dragon!" Trix screamed.

"Where?" one head asked to the sky.

"*FLEE!*" cried the second head with its eyes squeezed shut.

The third head said nothing. It looked asleep. Trix realized that it might be the one they had referred to as dead. How sad.

"Aren't you a dragon?" Trix asked the heads.

"Heavens no, child." The middle head laughed in relief.

"We are a lingworm," said the first head.

"I am Trix," said Trix. "It's a pleasure to meet you. Forgive me for not bowing before a being of such legendary grandeur, but my body seems to be on the outs with me at the moment."

"So polite," said the middle head. "Isn't that nice?"

"It would be nicer if he could get to the point," said the first head. Both were covered in curved indigo spikes, some of which remained taut as the heads conversed, and some of which flowed in the air above them like the plumes of an impressive bird.

"Forgive me," said Trix. "Is there some way I can help you?"

"Yes," said the first head.

"Thank you, dearie," said the middle head.

"Do you have a knife?" asked the first head.

Trix wasn't sure how to answer. He'd had quite a few things when he'd left the towerhouse the previous evening, but he hadn't been conscious for long enough yet to make an inventory of what was left on his person. He did that now. His sea star friend had returned home, it seemed, as had that pesky vision of his birthmother. He was also missing one shoe, the sack he'd prepared with extra bread and clothes, and his lucky four-leafed clover. But he still had his wits, the scar on his finger where he'd pricked himself on Sunday's spinning wheel, and the small dagger in his belt.

"I do have a knife," Trix answered with confidence.

"Good," said the first head. "We need you to chop off our dead Wisdom."

Trix was fairly sure his ears were still stopped up with magic ocean water, because he couldn't have heard that right. "I'm sorry, you want me to do what?"

"You're terrible," the middle head said to the first. "We've only just met, and it's a ghoulish thing you've asked him to do."

The first head sighed in exasperation. "We caught him in the Deep when he slipped off that leatherback in the current, and we carried him in our crest all night, until we reached this shore."

"Thank you," said Trix, grateful that the fallen sea star's gift had lasted well beyond his conscious state.

"You're welcome, dearie," said the middle head.

"He is a boy who can do things that need to be done," said the first head, as if it had never been interrupted. "This is something that needs to be done."

"I will help you if I can." Trix slid the dagger out of his belt; the small blade had been well protected by the sheath Saturday had fashioned for it. Trix made to polish it on his trousers, but hesitated when he realized his clothes were completely covered in layers of muck and slime.

"See?" said the first head. "He's rethinking it already."

"It's a lot to ask," said the middle head.

"I'm not sure I understand," said Trix. The mud drying on his face made his cheeks stiff as he spoke. "What exactly is it that you're asking?"

"What do you know about lingworms?" asked the first head.

Trix shrugged. "I thought you were a dragon."

"And you scared me half to death!" said the middle head. "Dragons haven't been around for ages."

"Neither have lingworms," said Trix. "At least, not around

here. But there's usually not an ocean around here either." He swung his arm to indicate the unharvested hayfield.

"Pitiable, uneducated youngling," said the first head.

"You have our sympathies," said the middle head.

The first head straightened his neck tall, as if it were sitting upright and not attached to a long, segmented body that sprawled and curled around itself for a hundred feet. It spoke as if reading from a book. "The legendary lingworm dwells deep beneath the Seven Seas. There are few descriptions of this serpent, because spotting it is so rare."

"'Tis luck to look on a lingworm," said the middle head. "That's what the sailors always say."

"The lingworm has three heads," the first head continued. "A Head of Truth, a Head of Compassion, and a Head of Wisdom."

The middle head tutted over the third, lifeless face with its spikes limply splayed on the ground. "Poor Wisdom."

"Should any one of the lingworm's heads be removed, it will grow back," said Truth. "Only by removing all three heads can the lingworm be killed."

"What a horrible thing to imagine," said Compassion. A shudder echoed down the segmented length of the sea serpent.

Trix heard this all as very good news. "Then you have nothing to worry about! Your Wisdom will grow back, maybe even better than before."

"Only it has to be removed first," Truth repeated.

"He's right, actually," said Compassion. "He usually is."

"Oh," said Trix. He looked at the very large head and very large neck of the very large sea serpent, and then down at his very small dagger. "This is not going to be pleasant."

"I imagine not," said Compassion.

"But it needs to be done," said Truth.

Somehow, Trix forced his sore body to stand. Broken shafts of hay stabbed into the pad of his shoeless foot. Each head of the lingworm towered above him, almost as tall as the trees in the Wood with those enormous plumes. Truth and Compassion looked back at him with eyes as big as his head, their matching irises as deep and green and cloudy as the deep and green and cloudy sea. Trix told himself to walk over to the fallen head, but himself would not obey.

"I'm afraid," he explained to the heads. "You are a very large beast, and I'm a very small boy."

"We will promise not to bite you or swallow you whole, or swat you with our tail," said Truth.

"Yes," said Compassion. "We promise."

The lingworm waved the end of the tail in question—the indigo spikes there were tipped with wicked barbs. Trix was not inspired by this. But the lingworm *had* carried him safely to the shore. To refuse performing a kindness in return would upset the balance of the universe, and the universe had enough of an upset goddess already.

"I will do this," he told his body more than the lingworm.

"Thank you," said Truth.

"Thank you," said Compassion.

Trix took a breath, held it, and then plunged his dagger deep into the giant neck of the lingworm. He was glad then that he'd held his breath, for the odor that released from the dead Wisdom was fetid and foul. When Trix finally was forced to take a breath, he choked and gagged.

"See?" said Truth. "You are still alive."

"You live up to your legend," Trix said to the lingworm. He scraped a few scales aside and plunged the dagger into the sea serpent's flesh again. It wasn't too different from cleaning a fish, he thought, if the fish were as big as a horse.

"So do you," Compassion replied, just as Trix hit his first vein. Sluggish golden blood welled up out of the ragged tear he'd made in Wisdom's neck and spilled over his hands.

"Wait," "said Trix. "You've heard of *me?*"

"The Lingworth are old enough to know the prophecies of this world, clever enough to remember them, and wise enough to have created a few ourselves," said Truth.

"There are few who do not know of The Boy Who Talks to Animals," said Compassion. "It is a tale that beasts have passed on to their children, and their children's children, throughout time. It was a story told before gods were gods."

The gods had been something else before being gods? The thought baffled Trix, but not half as much as the thought that no one else in the world had the same ability he had possessed all his life. "No one else can talk to animals?"

"Not to *all* the animals," said Truth.

"Not like you," said Compassion.

"What makes me so special?" asked Trix. It was a stupid

question. There were a lot of things that made him special. But he suspected he wasn't aware of just *how* special.

"Chaos is coming," said Truth.

"There is an imbalance in the world," said Compassion.

"I don't know that I'm special enough to set that to rights. You need someone more like my sister for that." Trix didn't specify which sister—for a boy with seven extraordinary sisters, it didn't really matter.

"Oh, the world will need your sisters, too," said Truth.

"There are prophecies enough for everyone!" cheered Compassion.

"But you will need to be the voice of the animals," said Truth. "It's a very important job."

"Be careful who you tell," said Compassion. "Men have been committed to slavery for far less."

"And still are," added Truth.

"And still are," said Compassion.

Trix was sorry now that Wisdom had not survived, for he would have liked that head's advice on what to do in his current situation. But if Wisdom had survived, Trix would not be in this current situation, and he would not know that the animals had been talking about him behind his back for centuries upon centuries upon... How long had the gods been gods, anyway? Not that it mattered. Everything happened for a reason, just like Mama always said.

At a loss, Trix concentrated on finishing his task. His dagger disappeared into the golden mess over and over again, blindly hacking into the stinky dead flesh with the goal of simply making it through to the other side. The sun continued to rise and Trix began to sweat into the lingworm's blood and flesh as he stepped further and further inside the carcass (losing his one remaining shoe in the process). When his right arm began to fail him, he sliced with his left, again and again and again. When he encountered bone, he pushed his body into the worm's neck with all his weight until he heard a *crack*. And just when he began to lose hope of ever finishing, the head of Wisdom fell away before him.

Truth and Compassion cheered. Trix might have too, but for the golden blood that now covered him in yet another layer from head to toe.

"Now take Wisdom back to the ocean," said Truth. "You must carry him as we carried you for a time."

One good turn deserved another. That was not something Mama always said, but it should have been. Trix wove his hands deep into the hairs that covered the top and back of Wisdom's head, mindful of the deadly indigo spikes there. The hairs were soft and hollow, crushing beneath his fingers as he found purchase in the locks. Where they bent, the indigo disappeared from the shafts, leaving them colorless. It made Trix think of the ink the great squid had released, and of his poet sister, Wednesday, with her penknife always at hand. This much ink in this many quills would have set her up forever. It was almost a shame to toss it into the sea. Perhaps, with luck, the damaged head would find its way to Faerie, where Wednesday played apprentice with their Aunt Joy. Wednesday would know what to do with it. Wednesday would not be afraid. In Trix's eyes, Wednesday had more Wisdom than this head could ever hold.

The head of Wisdom was heavy and unwieldy. Step by slow step, he dragged it with him into the sea.

"Wash yourself, Golden Boy," said Compassion.

"You're fey enough to live a long life without the help of our blood," said Truth.

The lingworm's words continued to baffle Trix. No one could know how long anyone might live, but then, he'd have thought no one could know he was going to exist once upon a time ago. Or better, know that he could talk to animals. Why hadn't all the animals he'd played with as a child told him this before?

Trix had thought to heave the head over his shoulder and into the surf, but the reality of that plan proved impossible. Trix dragged the head behind him into the sea until it was deep enough in the water to lead the way. Trix let Wisdom pull him under a bit before allowing the head to roll away, down the rest of the hill that used to be a hayfield, to the bottom of this magical ocean, wherever that used to be.

If this ocean ever went away again, some farmer was going to find quite a surprise in his yard. Goodness...what would Mama say? Thankfully, if this chaos had consumed the towerhouse, then his haphazard wish had saved the Woodcutters as well. He silently thanked the gods once more. He hoped they weren't tired of hearing from him.

Trix flipped and dove in the waves, swimming strong, as the fish in the river had taught him to swim. (Not like the fish in the cow pond had taught him, for they were lazy.) He shook vigorously, darting in and out through the underwater hay in an effort to clean himself. As he came back to shore he rubbed at his skin, making sure every speck he could reach was free of blood and mud. His mind might not be settled inside, but his body could be clean on the outside.

As Trix walked back to the lingworm through the new tidal surf, something bumped into his bare ankle. He reached down and pulled up what looked like a long, white stone. Upon further examination, he realized it was the point of a tooth. The only animal he'd ever met with a mouth this large was the lingworm, so it must have come from Wisdom.

"And so we send the dead to sea," said Truth.

"Whatever comes back to us is what they wish us to have," said Compassion.

"I should keep this?" asked Trix.

"Yes," said Truth. "It will help you on your travels."

"Whenever you need advice," said Compassion. "Wisdom is very helpful that way." The head looked down at the neighboring neck-stump, already sealing over nicely with a thin violet skin.

"You should also keep your dagger," said Truth.

Trix had not intended to dispose of his dagger, though he hadn't considered what effect the lingworm's blood would have on the blade. He pulled it from his belt and wiped at the gold blood with the bottom of his wet shirt. He wiped and wiped until he realized that there was no blood; the blade and hilt had turned completely gold.

"That blade will now cut through anything," said Truth, "and nothing born of earth can destroy it."

"Have a care not to lose it," said Compassion.

"Thank you," said Trix. While he wasn't sure yet how he might put Wisdom's tooth to use, the dagger was an instant treasure.

"It was a pleasure meeting you, Boy Who Talks to Animals," said Truth, and Trix took pride in the compliment.

"We look forward to telling the King of the Sea about you," said Compassion. "We are honored to have been part of your story."

With a flip and a roll powered by energy that Trix would not have believed the injured lingworm to have, the sea serpent slipped through the hay and disappeared into the waves of the magical ocean with fluid ease.

"So am I," Trix said to the vanished legend, equally as honored by the experience. "So am I."

4

The Golden Girl

ow fully awake and no longer deterred by the rich stink of golden lingworm blood, Trix's stomach growled. Judging by the sun, it had been the better part of a day since he'd eaten anything that hadn't been magically poisoned. What food he'd brought with him had been lost with his sack in the impossible ocean. He stood amidst a sea of tall hay that wouldn't prove much for him in the way of sustenance, but where there was a hay field, there was usually a farmer. A lazy farmer, judging by the state of this hay, but a farmer nonetheless. Making sure the golden dagger was securely fastened in his belt, Trix set off in the one direction that made sense: away from the ocean.

While Trix was not as tall as his sister Saturday (and probably never would be), the hay did not completely obstruct his view as he climbed the gently sloping hill. The field went on, unbroken, for miles. His stomach protested.

"There's no use getting all upset," Trix told his stomach. "It's not like there's another choice. We'll just have to walk until we find something."

Trix continued walking as promised, until his feet began to complain as well. This ground, untouched by magical waves, was cracked and dry and gray. Hay stalks that broke as he pushed through them, stabbing into the bottoms of his feet like tiny iron fire pokers.

"Sorry, feet," Trix said. "We can't rest until we find something to eat. But as soon as we do, we will rest for a very long time."

Trix kept up his pace, grumbling stomach and feet and all, across the endless hay field. The sun continued to rise in the cloudless sky as the sun does, clouds or not, and Trix's now-dry head and face began to burn.

"Stay sharp, head," Trix said to his overly warm pate. "Even if this hay would make a fine hat, we cannot stop until we find something to eat. When we do, we will eat and rest in the shade." Despite the pep talk his head continued to burn, hotter and hotter, so much so that he finally took his shirt off and wore it as a very limp hat.

All the while, Trix walked on, up and down the rolling hills, with nothing for miles in any direction but hay. When he got to the top of a particularly steep hill, he realized that the endless hay was an illusion. There, nestled in a small valley between two hay-covered hills, was a small cottage. Outside the small cottage was a giant apple tree, filled with apples. Trix's head and stomach and feet all cheered.

He took the measure of the cottage as he raced down the hill toward it. The grass on the paths around it was overgrown. The sod on the roof was sprinkled with wildflowers. No smoke rose from the chimney. No window or door, even on this beautiful day, was open. Trix decided that the cottage was abandoned, which explained the neglected hayfields. This was good news, for it meant all the apples he could eat and all the rest and shade he could soak up before continuing his journey onward. Oh, happy day!

Trix reached the bottom of the hill and stretched his arm out for the lowest, ripest apple on the tree.

"*Who comes to steal my apples?*"

The voice was female, slightly crackled with cold or age. The front door of the cottage was now open a crack. The voice had come from the darkness inside.

Trix bowed low to the cottage. "Trix Woodcutter, milady. I am but a poor boy journeying alone to an abbey in the north. My belongings were swept away in the magical sea. I thought this cottage abandoned, or I would never have presumed to take an apple from your tree without asking. That said, you do have many fine apples here. Could I trouble you for one or two of them, please, and the use of your tree's shade to rest my weary bones?"

"You may have as many apples as you desire," said the voice, "and you may rest as long as you like. But I would first have you do something for me."

Trix bowed again. His stomach growled mightily at the teasing abuse. "Name your task, milady."

"You must fetch me the topmost apple on that tree and bring it to me."

What luck! Having grown up next to the Wood, Trix was a master at climbing trees. He could do it in his sleep (and *had* on a few occasions, according to Sunday). This full tree, thick with branches, would be nothing at all for him to scale. "I will have your prize in the jiffiest of jiffs," Trix declared, and he quickly scrambled up the tree. As he leapt from limb to limb, he was so happy to be somewhere familiar that his aching head and feet and stomach forgot to complain.

In the jiffiest of jiffs his head emerged from the branches and leaves at the very top of the tree. From this vantage point, the white-capped mountains in the distance were larger than he'd ever seem them before; the magical ocean had taken him much farther north than he'd anticipated. A fortunate bit of chaos, that. A shorter journey was always good, once the worst obstacles had been cleared.

Not forgetting his task, he looked about to see which apple hung highest on the branches around him. There were plenty of apples here as well, but surely one must stand out...*a-ha!* He spotted it at once: a perfectly shaped apple made of solid gold. It snapped right off into Trix's hand as if it had been waiting to be plucked. Prize obtained, Trix slid down the branches and hopped down to the ground in a shower of leaves.

He bowed again, offering the fruit in his outstretched palm. Its weight reminded him of a certain golden ball his sister had been forced to sell at the market once…a bauble given to her with love by a frog who would be king. "Your apple, milady."

The door opened. Before him stood not the old witch he'd expected but a young woman. She was gold from head to toe. Her hair was gold. Her eyes were gold. Her clothes were gold. In the bright light of the sun he could even make out a small gold star in the middle of her forehead. Stunned by her blinding beauty he bent further, lowering his face to the ground.

"Would you share the apple with me, good Trix?" Her voice cracked again and she coughed daintily. Out here, all alone… Trix imagined this girl spoke to no one regularly, not even herself (which was a shame).

"But of course," said Trix. He unsheathed his lingworm-blessed dagger, golden as the apple in his hand. Putting it to the test, he set the blade to the cold metal surface. The flesh of the fruit parted easily for the dagger. Oh, happy day! The bright smell of deliciously ripe apple filled the air. Trix's stomach did somersaults in appreciation.

Papa was far better at slicing apples in midair than he. Trix had been a little more successful cutting off the head of the lingworm. The two pieces he now held were woefully unequal.

Trix's stomach took the opportunity to weigh in on the decision before him. *Take the larger half*, his stomach growled. *You're starving.*

Take the larger half, his feet winced. *You're tired.*

Take the larger half, said his head. *You deserve it. You've come such a long way, and you still have so far to go.*

And then suddenly, unexpectedly, the voice in his mind was that of Saturday. "GIVE HER THE LARGER HALF!" cried his warrior sister. Her words were hollow and felt far away, as far away as a towerhouse on a magical ocean, but they rang across the distance clear as a bell.

Oh, Saturday. How I miss you.

Trix smiled. All the voices were right. But this golden girl had promised him all the apples he wanted. Just because this particular apple was gold didn't make him want it any more than the plain old red and green ones still hanging happy and fresh on the tree behind him. Trix held his hands out to the girl, offering her both halves of the golden apple.

"For you, milady," he said. "The humble apples on yonder tree are more than enough for a poor Woodcutter like me."

There was a singing in the air that sounded like a swarm of bees, a riot of cicadas, and a sword being unsheathed all at once. The girl grinned at him with a smile as bright as the sun, and then flung herself into his arms. He had expected her movements to be stiff as a moving statue's and not quite so effervescently fluid, but there she was in the blink of an eye. Her enthusiasm reminded him of Friday, unabashedly throwing love around for all to share. He braced himself as he would have for one of Friday's hugs, which was good, because this girl did seem to *weigh* as much as someone who'd been dipped in gold.

"Thank you!" she cried. "Thank you for releasing me from my spell!"

She smelled of honeysuckle and smoke, delicious scents than

made Trix's stomach churn in frustration. The girl must have heard it for she released him soon after, walking over to the tree and picking a shiny red and green apple for him.

"For those vociferous hollows," she told him. Her voice was stronger now, though her skin and eyes and skirts and hair were no less golden.

"That and twenty more like it, with great thanks." Trix greedily took the apple from her and bit into its tart flesh.

"All you need is one," she said. "You'll see."

She spoke truly. By the time Trix finished the apple, he felt as fat as a pig before Midwinter Feast. "Thank you, milady," he said as he wiped the juice from his chin.

"Please call me Lizinia," she told him. "You also wanted to rest in the shade of my tree. Join me here and I will tell you my story." She spread her golden skirts and sat gracefully on the ground beside the apple tree. Trix didn't have Friday's eye for material, but he'd never before seen metal move like silk, no matter how finely hammered.

Oh, Friday. How I miss you.

Shade and stories…Trix sighed. This was almost like being at home, except that his family's clothing wasn't half so fine. "Should I fetch you a blanket?" he asked. "Aren't you worried you'll muss your splendid dress?"

She laughed again and her golden fingers flew to her golden cheeks, as if the act of laughing itself was foreign to her. "My clothes can never wear or tear or stain," she told him. "Nor can anyone else remove them but me. That is part of my story."

Satisfied, Trix settled back against the trunk of the tree. He gazed up into its thick leaves, bright and green with sunlight. His stomach and feet and head quieted as he settled in to hear Lizinia's tale.

"I haven't always lived in this cottage," she began. "I grew up in an old house not far from here, with my mother and older sister Peppina."

"Where was your father?" Trix asked lazily.

"Mother told us that he died when we were very young," said Lizinia.

"You sound dubious."

"Mother was not known for being truthful. Or generous. Mine was a happy, humble life, but in Mother's eyes we were destitute and deserving of so much more."

"And your sister?"

"My sister, unfortunately, took after our mother. She dreamed of places she would never live and riches she would never own and men she would never marry. Then she would get mad because she didn't have those things."

"She must have been mad a lot," said Trix.

"They both were. And so I spent my sunny days working in the garden and playing with the birds and squirrels and rabbits who came to visit me. They cared only for kindness and did not mind my humble trappings."

"As it should be." Trix made the comment in a low voice, so as not to disturb the natural rhythm of his new friend's narrative. Just as Papa had taught him.

"On rainy days, I cleaned the house. At night, I would cook dinner and tend to the mending. I had peace of mind, but nothing was ever enough for my mother and sister. So when the cats offered to pay my mother in exchange for my servitude, I went with them freely."

"Cats?" Even with his fantastic talent, Trix had always been leery of cats. Cats could see things most humans and many fey could not. They were not always wise beyond their years, but they acted as if they possessed the knowledge of the ages. Worst of all, they spoke—when they wanted to be heard—in riddles that could drive even the most fey-blessed denizens of the Wood mad with frustration.

Lizinia indicated the small cottage beside them. "There were dozens of them, maybe even a hundred, and I was brought here to live with them. I cared for them: made their meals, washed their sheets, and kept the house in order. The only difference from my old life was that I had more free time to myself."

"And no grouching at every turn," said Trix. "It sounds rather nice."

"It was." Lizinia leaned back against the trunk of the tree as well, her voice dreamy with memory. "A full year went by before I began to miss my old bed, my old garden, and my mother and sister. Since it had been a successful year, Papa Gatto felt that I had more than earned my keep, so he let me return home."

"Papa Gatto?"

"Papa Gatto was the leader of the cats, the wisest and most powerful of them all. It was he who hired me, and thusly he who rewarded me for my service."

Lizinia touched the star on her golden forehead, her golden cheek, her golden dress in wistful thought. Trix didn't have to ask her the extent of Papa Gatto's reward. "Was it scary, being dipped in gold?"

"A little," she admitted. "Thank you. No one has ever asked me that. But then, no one before has offered me the golden apple either."

"Did they eat it?" asked Trix.

"No," said Lizinia. "They would steal it, or try to melt it down. Those that melted the apple were left with ashes, or dust, or a pile of fragrant mush."

"And those that stole the apple?"

Lizinia shrugged. "Nothing pleasant, I imagine, but I never followed them to learn. Per Papa Gatto's instructions, once a visitor failed the test, I closed the door and locked it tight. Another golden apple always appeared on the tree the very next day."

"Good," said Trix. Those greedy gobs deserved whatever they got. "So what did your mother say when you returned home looking like...that?"

"She was overjoyed, as you can imagine. Until she realized that she could not cut my hair, or remove my apron, or take off my shoes. All of this gold at her fingertips, and none of it hers! She locked me in a cupboard, and then told Peppina to go to the cats' cottage and offer herself up for servitude."

"I'm going to guess that didn't go well," said Trix.

"You guess rightly. To Peppina, cats were pompous, smelly

animals that made her itch. Not that it mattered—had they been unicorns, lazy Peppina wouldn't have served them for more than five minutes. It wasn't two weeks before Papa Gatto offered to release her from her contract and send her home. Thinking she was going to be rewarded as I had been, Peppina let herself be dipped in a vat of pitch."

"Ouch," said Trix, thinking more of the sister's pride than pain.

"It got worse. She did not follow Papa Gatto's precise directions on how to return home. By the time she arrived, a donkey's tail had sprouted from her forehead." Lizinia pointed to the star on her own brow.

"Oh no." Trix had made many mistakes in his life; he couldn't imagine having to wear his shame so blatantly.

"Oh, *yes*. Peppina went out of her selfish mind with grief. Mother was beside herself. Neither of them could bear to look at me after that, so they threw me out of the house. I ran away— here—the only other home I have ever known. Papa Gatto graciously took me in. I went on to care for him and the rest of the cats for the whole of their lives."

"Are there none still living?" asked Trix.

"No." There was sorrow in her eyes. "This cottage was where they all came to live out the twilight of their ninth life after the first eight had been spent. Because of the wisdom and power that he held, Papa Gatto was the last to go. He put a spell on the cottage that gave me everlasting life, until someone finally came along who was worthy of my goodness. Only then would I be allowed to leave this place and travel as I chose. This apple tree was both my sole sustenance, and my sole means of escape. Papa Gatto promised to always be there for me, to guide me on my way." She squinted up into the leaves above Trix's head. "I can almost see him up there in the branches of this apple tree, smiling down upon us. I think he is happy that you have come at long last. As am I."

"Cats can smile?" Trix asked playfully.

Lizinia turned her body to face him. "Trix Woodcutter, may I accompany you on your journey?"

"I am going to see my mother."

"I would love to meet her," said Lizinia.

"She is dead." Papa told him it was always best to be honest.

"All the more reason that you should not travel alone," said Lizinia. "I will accompany you to the grave of your mother, and we may decide from there whether to companion each other further. Do we have a deal?"

It was a fairer offer than most of his other siblings would suggest.

"Adventure awaits!" said Trix. He spat in his palm and held his hand out for Lizinia to shake. She did, her warm metal hand slipping into his.

As soon as their palms touched, the tree above them began to shake. Apples flew everywhere, pummeling both Trix and Lizinia, and Trix did not have the benefit of golden armor to protect him. The blue sky was devoid of clouds and yet the tree bent and waved wildly, as if belatedly tossed in the magical storm Trix had left behind the night before. The cottage, too, was suddenly abuzz with movement. Shutters clattered against the window panes. The door opened wide and slammed shut nine times in quick succession.

The tenth time the door opened, Lizinia gasped.

"What?" Trix asked the golden girl. "What's happening?"

"Papa Gatto." Her eyes were wide. "Did you not see him walk through the door?"

"I saw nothing," Trix said in earnest, but he had enough experience in an enchanted Wood to know that didn't necessarily mean nothing was there to see. Especially when it had to do with cats.

Lizinia slowly turned her head to Trix. "Papa Gatto would like you to go inside."

That hadn't been a daunting prospect before the empty house had come alive on its own. "Am I to be dipped in oil? Peanut butter? A vat of snakes?"

"I don't know," said Lizinia. "No other traveler has passed the test before."

"Well done, me," Trix said to himself. And then to Lizinia, "Any advice you'd care to impart would be greatly appreciated in this moment."

"Just be careful. Be kind. Be wise." She picked a shiny apple off the ground and tossed it to him. "Be yourself."

The front door of the cottage loomed before him. Even with all the talents he possessed, he wasn't sure he had what it took to stand up to a Cat Lord and declare his intentions toward his goddaughter. As he exhaled, Trix boldly walked up the stoop and lifted his fist to knock. Silently, the door slid open a crack, as if anticipating his entry.

"Adventure awaits," he whispered, and stepped inside.

5

The Grinning Cat

he door slammed behind Trix.

There was no wind.

He took a deep breath—the air did not possess that stale tang of old silence. It smelled instead as Lizinia did, of honeysuckle and banked embers. His eyes searched the shadows. The main living area was spacious. Couches and chairs formed a circle around a grand fireplace—every one of them soft and inviting. Even the rug looked comfortable. There was a small piano and several stout bookcases—the cats could read? Or they had been collected for Lizinia, who had been trapped with them inside this cozy prison for who knew how long. Trix bet she could quote every page from memory.

Not a lamp was lit, not a candle flickered. An alcove in the back seemed to lead to the kitchen and, presumably, the living quarters and the rest of the house. Light from the—now unshuttered— windows filled the main room, but Trix could not see beyond the dark doorway. And nowhere was there a cat to be found.

"Come to the light, boy."

The words were wheezy like an errant breeze. The wall immediately to Trix's left had two large windows. Each cast an equally large rectangle of light onto the floorboards before it. Trix squinted into the farthest rectangle, catching the faintest flicker of dust motes in the sun's rays at the edge of his vision. Bit by bit, the sparkles of light resolved themselves into a squat, puffy shape.

Be it this life or the next, Trix thought to himself. *Cats do prefer the sunny spots.*

The spectral feline groomed himself, his flattened face making barely a dent in the voluminous fluff of his coat. His fur reminded Trix of smoke from wet wood or storm clouds, both black and white, the shades of gray between them soft and threatening. Just like smoke and clouds, Papa Gatto's form seemed to shift in and out of tangibility.

Trix boldly stepped forward into the closest rectangle of light. Papa Gatto might have intended the intense rays of the afternoon to add to the feeling of scrutiny, but Trix felt safe in the sun. He clasped his hands behind his back as Mama had taught him— fiddling fingers were distracting, she said, and made boys look idle.

Mama had also taught Trix the importance of speaking only when spoken to, in such situations. As Trix waited in that silent square of sun, he came to the conclusion that it wouldn't be unusually rude of him to get on with the conversation, so long as he'd already been spoken *at*.

"It is an honor to meet you…" Trix knew this was Papa Gatto but suddenly felt odd speaking so familiarly. How might the departed patriarch like to be addressed? Trix considered what he knew of cats and went with "…your majesty."

Papa Gatto ceased his constant cleansing and looked up at the address. His head was wider than the cats Trix had encountered in the Wood, his ears more gently curved than pointed and set far apart. His muzzle was also far less pronounced. His whiskers pulled down both sides of his mouth, giving the impression of jowls and a permanently stern look, as if he were unhappy with everything. Lizinia had mentioned that Papa Gatto had grinned down at her beneath the apple tree, but Trix honestly couldn't imagine this cat ever cracking a smile.

The smoky fur was black as pitch around Papa Gatto's nose and mouth, a feature that enhanced the cat's large silver-green eyes. Trix had encountered mist that same color in the Wood and had avoided it along with the rest of the animals. Magic ran wild in that mist, adding an element of madness to everything it touched.

"What is your name, child?" the cat's words were a wheeze and a hiss, as if his voice, too, was only able to half-materialize in this world.

"Trix Woodcutter, your majesty." He bowed low.

Papa Gatto let out a mumbling rasp and coughed a little. Trix wondered what a semi-incorporeal hairball might look like. "Why did you, Trix Woodcutter, lie to my goddaughter Lizinia?"

Trix furrowed his brow. Of all the things he'd not expected the cat to say, this hadn't even made the list. Trix had been accused of many things in his life, but lying was not among them.

"Forgive me, your majesty, but...I don't actually know what you're talking about."

"I see all and know all," the cat said hoarsely. "Now more than ever."

Trix was happy for the cat's new abilities and appreciation of such, but he still didn't see what any of it had to do with him. Still, the cat seemed to be waiting for Trix to admit something. "Yes, sir." It was all he could think to say.

The cat sighed and shifted his fluid, ethereal girth. His long tail swept across the floor like Mama's mop, stirring more bright dust into the shaft of light around him. The edges of his soft coat faded in and out of existence. "You introduced yourself to Lizinia as 'a poor boy.'"

"But I *am* a poor boy," said Trix. "My family and I live in a humble cottage on the edge of the Wood." Assuming it was still there after the floodwaters rose. "There used to be a treehouse too, but it got swallowed by a beanstalk. We don't even have a cow because...well, I sold her and bought the beans that created the beanstalk." Trix continued to rack his brain. "Mama and Papa have a goose now that lays golden eggs, but I wouldn't say that classifies us as rich."

Papa Gatto coughed again, many times in succession. If the cat hadn't been dead already, Trix would have called out for help. And then he realized Papa Gatto was laughing. At him.

"You are yet a child, but I would never call you poor, Boy Who Talks to Animals."

"Ah. That." Perhaps if Lizinia had been an animal he might have introduced himself as such, not that he ever needed to, since this blasted prophetic reputation obviously proceeded him. "I've only been told that tale recently—it's definitely not how I think of myself. I would not presume a sophistication I do not feel I own."

A cloud moved over the sun; the cat faded out of existence and then back in as the shadow passed. When he spoke again he mumbled, as if his cheeks were filled with cotton. "You do think of yourself as a brother, do you not?"

"Seven times over," Trix said proudly.

"And who is your sister?"

Trix opened his mouth to ask the cat which sister he meant, and then shut it once more. From the way Papa Gatto had phrased the question, only one sister mattered. When Trix took a moment to think, he realized the answer was obvious. He exhaled in defeat. "The Queen of Arilland."

Which I reckon makes you a prince."

Trix shook his head. "That it does. But the title is still new to me—not so new as that other one, but new all the same. I do not live in the palace"—Trix shivered at the thought of being cooped up in a place like that, no matter how sprawling—"nor do I present myself as a prince to anyone. Ever."

The cat scoffed. "Prince or no, I cannot send my dear Lizinia off in the company of a liar."

Trix squinted at the cat. Papa Gatto's edges were fading again.

"With respect, your majesty, I don't believe that's your decision anymore."

Papa Gatto hissed and pranced about on his short legs. "Impudent scamp," he wheezed.

Trix pointed at the cat. "Now *that's* more like it. I've been called that often enough to answer to it when summoned." By Mama no less, and everything Mama said was true. "Surely a fine cat such as yourself can appreciate those qualities. You can't tell me you weren't an impudent scamp in any of your lives."

"In all of them," the cat rasped proudly. And then he did that thing Lizinia had sworn she'd witnessed under the apple tree: Papa Gatto grinned.

It was one of the most frightening sights Trix had ever seen.

"Well then, Trix Woodcutter. Now that the formalities are out of the way, you must prove to me that you are worthy of my goddaughter."

"I'm not sure that I can," said Trix.

"Then you must be unworthy," said the grinning cat.

"I'm worthy of a lot of things, your majesty," Trix countered. "I just don't know your goddaughter that well. We've only just met. I'd feel uncomfortable speaking on her behalf."

"Wise words from a body of so few years."

Trix slid his hand down to where the tooth of Wisdom rested in the crude pocket at the bottom of his shirt. Friday had altered a few of his shirts thusly so that he might collect certain herbs and stones and other precious trinkets while on his daily jaunts through the Wood. He was still not sure what use the trinket would be to him, but he was glad of its company all the same. "Thank you, your majesty."

Papa Gatto had not yet instructed him to drop the affectation so Trix maintained that overly polite air. He did notice a sound not unlike a gravelly purr coming from the spectral cat, and he took that as a good sign.

"All right then, Scamp. Let's measure your suitability, shall we?" Papa Gatto's face faded away momentarily, but Trix still nodded his readiness at the smoky ball of fur. "You do seem a bit scrawny."

"I'm not fully grown," said Trix, "and I have fey blood. It makes me look younger than I am."

The cat regarded him with those haunting green eyes as he faded in and out of sight. "Can you make a fire?" he asked when enough of his mouth returned to form words.

"Yes, your majesty," Trix said with confidence.

"Do you know which plants are poisonous and which are not?" asked the cat.

"I know of many," said Trix, "but I have not traveled the world enough to know them all. I trust the animals to let me know when I might be making the wrong decision."

Papa Gatto harrumphed his disdain. "Could you survive on your own with no help from animal friends?"

"I believe I could, but I hope I never have to find out." Trix narrowed his eyes at the cat. "I hope Lizinia never has to find out either."

Papa Gatto preened, a gesture that told Trix that the cat *did* intend to stay with Lizinia in spirit well beyond the confines of this cottage. "I would have you perform three tasks for me," the cat said, in between bouts of grooming his soft, smoky locks.

Trix resisted rolling his eyes at the ridiculous suggestion. What did his performing tasks have to do with Lizinia finally getting away from this comfortable prison the cats had forced upon her? But cats were cats, for better or worse, and as this particular cat seemed determined to stick with his goddaughter as long as possible, it couldn't hurt for Trix to keep things sailing smoothly for as long as possible. Trix knew enough about cats to know that if one of them wanted to make life difficult for you, you could end up wishing you'd never been born.

"What would you have of me, your majesty?"

A golden square of light appeared on the shadowed floor between them. "Take that magic cloth you see before you," said the cat. "I want you to clean this house from top to bottom."

Trix clenched his jaw, stepped forward, and lifted the rag. It was as insubstantial as the cat, its silvered edges fading whenever it lost the light. Trix wouldn't be cleaning anything with this! He looked around the cottage. The *spotless* cottage. He imagined Lizinia had little else to do in the countless years she'd been in residence.

"Yes, your majesty," Trix said into the bow. He raised the spirit-cloth high into the air and spun about, pantomiming a swipe across the windowsill and shutters directly to his left.

By the time Trix had pretended to clean the living area, Papa Gatto had begun to clean himself again. By the time Trix was done waving his arms around the kitchen, Papa Gatto had curled up into a fat, fluffy ball in his square of sunlight, snoring as he periodically winked in and out of oblivion. Trix took the opportunity to investigate the cottage in its entirety.

The bedrooms beyond the kitchen were small and equally clean as a whistle. Had he not heard the story from Lizinia herself, Trix would never have thought this place was once inhabited by a hundred cats. Nor was there much evidence that a girl lived here. There were no flowers in pots, no looms, no paints. No sticks, no stones, no pretty leaves nor fragrant herbs. Trix discovered no other instrument besides the piano in the front room. Trix had never before considered a life without mementos—now that he had, he deemed it a rather sad life indeed. More than ever he looked forward to traveling with Lizinia and introducing her to…well…everything.

There was no true "top" to the house but Trix found the bottom, through a small cellar door opposite the pantry. Even this room was spotless, every jar on every shelf arranged just so and turned so that the labels—written in Lizinia's very neat hand— were visible. There was an enormous vat where presumably the girls had been dipped in their deserved rewards. It was empty of either magical gold or magical pitch.

Even the feyest of cats had limitations, it seemed.

When Trix was through sating his curiosity, he made his way back up the stairs to where Papa Gatto still slumbered. Trix took his original spot in the other window's square of light, now slightly fading. He sat cross-legged on the floor and watch the cat a while.

Instead of Papa Gatto's image blurring at the edges, the outline of the cat seemed crisp and clear. It was the bulk of the animal that was hazy now, smoke curling in and around on itself to the sound of slow and even cat snores.

Trix let the magical dust cloth slip to the ground. "Finished!" he announced.

The cat snapped back into reality with a cough and a scowl. Trix tried to look a little less proud of himself than he was feeling. For an all-seeing, all-knowing entity, Papa Gatto didn't seem to be aware of how little dirt was in this place. Not that he would check anyway—Trix had a feeling that Papa Gatto could not travel beyond that square of light from which he currently reigned.

"Imp," said Papa Gatto.

"At your service, your majesty," said Trix. "What would you have me do next?"

"You must fluff the mattresses," the cat said without pause. "Beat them until the feathers fly." With a stretch and a yawn, he curled about himself and became smoke on a sunbeam once more.

Trix shrugged, got up, and walked back to the bedrooms. These must have been the tasks the cats had set to Lizinia and her sister all those years ago. A decent enough interview for a housemaid, perhaps, but none of this gave the cat an ability to gauge Trix's fitness for travel. Papa Gatto was playing with him, that was obvious, like a mouse on a string. And Trix didn't mind going through the motions, however ridiculous, he only wished he could peek his head out a window and keep Lizinia informed as to his status.

Trix shook out the mattresses and then reassembled them as they had been before. He collected the feathers and brought them back to the main room, where he dropped them in a quiet pile atop the magical dust cloth.

"Finished!" he exclaimed, and again the cat reappeared in a huff. "Scamp."

"That's 'Prince Scamp,' if you don't mind," Trix said playfully.

Unexpectedly, Papa Gatto did not frown at Trix's jest. No, the grin was back, as disconcerting as ever. The silver green eyes sparkled with delight. Three balls of yarn materialized on the floor before him.

"Your third and final task," said the cat. "You must choose which ball of yarn is my favorite."

Trix smirked. If the other two tasks had been senseless, this one was positively laughable. How in the world was Trix expected to choose the right one? And even if he did, who was to say that Papa Gatto wouldn't lie, or change his mind?

"What does it even matter, anyway?" Trix asked brazenly. "You cannot stop Lizinia from traveling with me, no more than you can stop the sun from shining right through you."

"Nor can I dip you in gold or pitch for your insolence." The cat's eyes seemed to glow brighter. Trix placed a hand over his chest, as if to keep his soul from being examined by those giant, haunting eyes. "But I have allies in the corporeal world, allies that can see that you find your way into a barrel full of snakes and boiling oil and never find your way out. You won't see my goddaughter—or anyone else—ever again." The grin returned, and it was just as terrifying as ever. "First rule of the forest, my boy: Never cross a cat."

The hairs on Trix's neck rose, and gooseflesh covered his arms. He knew that tone of voice—it was one Mama had only used on him once or twice before in his life. Trix had thought himself clever enough to call the spectral cat's bluff, but that raspy tenor meant business. Trix might not know when or how or by whom Papa Gatto's threat might be carried out, but it was indeed very real, and very hazardous to Trix's health.

It was time to call in reinforcements.

Trix pulled the tooth of Wisdom from his pocket.

Papa Gatto reared up on his short legs with a hiss. "Where did you get that?" he spat.

"From a friend," Trix said. He held the tooth out before the balls of yarn and said politely, "Dear Tooth, which of these is Papa Gatto's favorite?"

The tooth said nothing. The tooth did nothing. Trix moved in front of each one of the balls. He pointed the tooth at them. Waved the tooth above them.

Nothing.

Trix pursed his lips in thought a moment, and then came to a decision. "I can only conclude that your favorite ball of yarn is not among these," he said.

The tooth glowed at that, brighter than the afternoon sun's light. This time, it was Trix who smiled.

"Cheater!" wheezed the cat.

Trix slipped the tooth back into his pocket. "I do not believe it's cheating for me to use the tools I have at my disposal. In fact, I'd think less of me if I didn't use those tools. Wouldn't you?"

The cat huffed and preened.

"I thought so," said Trix.

"You may now claim your reward," the cat said, though Trix had no idea how. A cloud had gone over the sun. The words were there, but the cat wasn't. The cloud moved and the cat returned. Beside him was a small vial that looked as ghostly as its giver.

Trix picked up the vial. It was made of light, weighing nothing and containing nothing. The label on the vial read *KanaLuna* in fading script. Trix had no idea what he was supposed to do with this gift, assuming it retained physical form once removed from the square of light cast by the window. "Um...thank you?"

"Drink," said the cat.

"But there's nothing in it," said Trix.

"Then you have nothing to fear."

Trix smirked at the cat, wishing nothing more than to be done with this nonsense so he and Lizinia could get on with their journey. He lifted the phantasmal vial to his lips and pretended to consume its absent contents. "Are we done now?"

The cat huffed again, and then grinned once more, baring all of those old, scary, pointed teeth. There were no blurred outlines here. "Cats are never done," he said, and then vanished into the light.

Trix waited a while, just to be sure the cat had disappeared for good. He threw open the front door to where Lizinia stood, a lovely statue of anticipation. "We are free to go!" he announced.

Instead of the enthusiastic response he expected, she tilted her head at him like a broken bit of clockwork. "Trix? Is that you?"

Girls did ask the strangest questions sometimes. "Of course it's me! You've been here the whole time. Did you see anyone else walk through this door?"

Lizinia tilted her head the other way. Raising her eyebrows, she looked him over from head to toe. "It's just…" She squinted at his face. "You look…taller."

Trix straightened proudly at the compliment. Come to think of it, his shirt did feel a bit tighter around the chest and arms. Did that happen when one grew taller? His older brother Peter was as barrel-chested as Papa, which came from being a Woodcutter, but he wasn't as tall as, say, Saturday. Not that Peter was around to ask. "Well, it's still me, and I'm still anxious to get to Rose Abbey. You're still coming with me, right?"

The joy Trix had anticipated earlier returned to her face. Lizinia clapped her hands. "Let me just collect a few things."

Trix moved to let her past him but he remained in the doorway, just in case Papa Gatto had any ideas of locking her up again. From the bedrooms, the golden girl fetched a cloak the color of the sky that covered her from head to toe. From the pantry, she fetched a satchel. "I thought we might collect some apples for our journey."

"Great idea," said Trix, happy that she was traveling light.

Lizinia paused on the threshold. She turned back to the main room and blew it a kiss before closing the cottage door, which she locked with a golden key that hung from a chain around her neck. Trix said nothing; he knew how difficult it was to leave one's home behind, prison or no.

"What should we do with this?" Trix asked of the golden apple he'd split in half. While they had prepared to leave it had turned solid metal, from the rind to the pips.

"Bring it," said Lizinia. She put the smaller half of the golden apple in the pocket of her cloak and handed the other half to Trix. "We might need to spend it on something."

"Thank you," said Trix.

"Not at all," said Lizinia. "Only…I do have a small favor to ask of you."

Trix bowed to her as he had to her godfather. Surely whatever she asked couldn't be as silly as anything Papa Gatto had invented "Name your task, milady."

He could not tell from the shadows cast by the hood of her cloak, but judging by her body language, his comment had left her blushing. (Trix certainly had enough sisters to know.)

"Before we start on the journey to your mother, would you please take me to this 'magical sea' that you spoke about? I have never seen the sea, magical or otherwise."

It was miles out of their way, back over the hills and through the never-ending hayfields. Trix looked up at the sky, noted the position of the sun, and assessed their bearings.

"This way!" he said excitedly. Because no matter where they went, at least they were *going*. There were no clouds in the sky: neither storms nor cats would cause any more mischief this day.

Trix was happy to note that his enthusiasm pleased Lizinia. Obligingly, she followed him through the hay. "So what did you and Papa talk about?"

"Oh, all sorts of things," said Trix. "I don't expect we'll ever be the best of friends, but we worked it out. And I didn't end up dipped in anything, which I consider a triumph. Mostly I was relieved when he stopped being mad at me. He really does grin, doesn't he? That's a strange sight."

"Mad? Whyever was Papa Gatto mad at you?"

"Because I forgot to tell you I was a prince. Come on, now, keep up. Adventure awaits!"

6

The True Story

rix and Lizinia made their way east along the edge of where the impossible ocean met the land it had swallowed. Lizinia kept her hood up, even in the heat of midday, to avoid the urges of any greedy passersby who might want to steal her for themselves. Not that they had encountered anyone as of yet, but Trix was thankful for the gesture as well. He found he liked to look at people when he spoke to them. When Lizinia faced the sun, any conversation was positively blinding.

They took turns carrying the sack of apples they had collected—it remained heavy, as they each needed only one a day to stay energized. When they stopped to rest, Lizinia wove a sturdy chain of daisies and vines from which Trix could hang Wisdom's tooth around his neck. It had not yet ceased to amaze Trix how nimble her small fingers were, despite the fact that they looked to be made of solid gold.

"You're very good at that," he said, when he remembered that Mama had advised him it was not polite to stare. "My sister Friday would like you. She's deft with a needle. And weaving. And mending. And pretty much anything else that involves laundry."

"You mention your sisters a lot," said Lizinia.

Trix shrugged. "Hard to avoid, what with there being seven of them and all."

The golden girl smiled—her teeth, like her eyes, had not been coated in the cats' magic metal. "The way you talk about them, though...the tone of your voice, the look on your face...you all must love each other very much."

"We do," he said. The guilt of poisoning Mama, Papa, Saturday and Peter rose up in his stomach again and the shame left a bitter taste in his throat. He did not yet feel comfortable confessing this transgression to Lizinia. Thankfully, she had not asked why none of his family accompanied him on this trip. Trix pushed the terrible feeling aside and tried not to think about it.

"So...Sunday is good with words. Saturday is a hard worker. Friday is good at sewing." Lizinia pulled a knot tight and moved onto the rest of the plait. "What are you good at?"

"Making messes," Trix said proudly.

Lizinia looked up at him. Her irises held an amber hue and Trix wondered if they had been that color all along, or if they had been changed by the magic gold as well. "You shouldn't do that," she said.

He'd been so caught up in imagining what Lizinia had looked like before her gold bath that he didn't hear exactly what she'd said, but Trix was familiar enough with the women in his family to recognize a scolding tone. "Do what?"

"Talk about yourself like you're a pest," she said. "Do you honestly think you're such a horrible person?"

"No," Trix said with a little less confidence. "Of course not."

"Do your brothers and sisters call you names?"

"We're siblings," said Trix. "We're always calling each other names. No harm is ever meant by it. It's all in good fun."

"Peppina used to call me horrible names," said Lizinia. "Mama too. They also said it was 'in good fun.' Only I was not the one having fun."

Trix noticed that her hands had begun to tremble. He took them in his own, as he would have had she been any of his other sisters. (Except maybe Saturday, who was careful to never show weakness.) "My family is kind, Lizinia. We are loud and messy and we make up stories and we call each other names. We work and we play and we eat and we love and we have great adventures. It's a good family. You would like them. And they would love you, just as they love me."

"But do you love yourself?"

"I..." It wasn't a question anyone had asked Trix before, and so it was nothing he'd ever previously considered. It was true, he *was* good at making messes, better than anyone else he knew. And he rather enjoyed the results of those predicaments, be they disastrous or otherwise. He was a Woodcutter, after all: adventure was in his blood. "I believe I do. Do you?"

"I don't know," she said softly. "I don't think so." Her voice wavered.

"If you cry, are your tears water or gold?"

Lizinia's shock at the question distracted her from her sadness, as Trix had hoped it would. "I don't know. I haven't had cause to be sad for a long time. Wistful, maybe. Lonely. But not sad."

"Good. Stay not sad." Trix squeezed her hands. "And don't worry. I will love you."

"You will?"

Trix nodded as solemnly as a soldier going into battle. "As if you were one of my very own sisters. How about that?"

"I would like that," said Lizinia. "But don't start calling me names right away, if you please. I may have to work up to that."

"As you wish, Princess Shining Star. Oops! Sorry. Won't happen again."

Lizinia cocked her head. "Well, that one wasn't so—"

"No!" Trix put a hand over his heart. "You made me swear not to call you names, milady, and so I shall not, until you give me leave to do so once more."

"*Now* you sound like a prince."

"Ugh." Trix pulled a face that made Lizinia laugh. "It's not my fault I'm a prince. I'm just a boy."

"Well then, you are a funny boy, Trix Woodcutter."

"I am a funny boy who excels at making messes."

"Indeed," said Lizinia. "Well, then. I suppose I'll just have to stick around to see these messes for myself. Who knows? You might excel at a few other things you're not even aware of."

"I hope I do, milady."

Lizinia smiled as she shook her head, in that exasperated way all his sisters did, and Trix knew that everything would be fine.

"You know," she said as she wound the thin, supple vines around the largest part of the tooth, "we should cut the golden apple into smaller chunks. That way, when we need to spend it on something, we won't be flashing all our funds in front of whoever we're bartering with."

"We'd also be less likely to get cheated," said Trix. "When a vendor knows you have money, they don't knock their prices down as much."

"Learned that the hard way, did you?"

Trix grinned. "One day, I was at the market haggling over magic beans to keep my family from starving. The next, I was handed a bunch of royal tokens and told to buy anything I wanted. A strange juxtaposition, to be sure. But one that supports your theory. Look, the tooth agrees with you."

Wisdom's tooth glowed a happy rose color, deeming Lizinia's plan to chop up the golden apple a wise one. Trix was starting to enjoy having the tooth around...when it didn't remind him of Mama. Already it had warned him against venturing back into the sea, and climbing a tree near the edge of a cliff to look for bird's eggs, and walking on slick rocks near a waterfall. Once he had introduced Lizinia to the tooth's properties, she went a little overboard seeking its advice. Trix had to stop her when she started asking it where to put one foot in front of the other. For a while, he worried that they'd never get to Rose Abbey before his mother was buried.

Trix pulled the golden dagger from his belt and shaved the golden apple down into smaller slices. Lizinia forced him to stop long enough to slip the necklace she had fashioned over his head.

"I'm going to collect firewood before it gets dark," she said. The tooth continued to shine, even after she'd let go.

"If you spend any more time with this thing, *you* are going to start glowing, Wise One."

Lizinia raised her finger at the name calling, but smiled as she turned and set to her chore.

Trix was far more accustomed to foraging in the Wood, so he had given Lizinia this easy task and left the hunting of edibles for himself. They would tire of the magic apples soon enough, and Trix didn't want to risk them accidentally ingesting something they shouldn't. He placed a hand over his stomach, remembering the horrible cramps the poison stew had given him. He'd certainly had enough difficulty in that area to last a lifetime.

A squirrel and a chipmunk obligingly led him to a thicket of ripe blackberries. Trix shoved enough berries into his mouth to stuff his cheeks as full as the chipmunk's, and then took off his shirt and collected scads more for Lizinia. The chipmunk also assisted with the location of a few root vegetables, while the squirrel showed Trix the path that led to a coven of wisps from whom they were able to steal fire without being detected.

Lizinia had accomplished her mission successfully. Trix returned to a bounty of firewood of varying thickness and length (the cats' blessing seemed to have made Lizinia at least as strong as Saturday, a useful asset). A pair of groundhogs made quick work of digging a pit, inside which Trix fashioned a square of larger wood full of twigs. He tilted three more sizable logs into a tower above the square, and then placed the wisps' light inside with the kindling. The wind was with them and the fire lit quickly and successfully. Trix thanked the Four Winds and the Fire Angels and the God of Travelers, making a mental note to acquire some more flint at the first opportunity.

The herd of deer they'd passed had told them it was but another day or so to the Abbey (given that humans were considerably slower than deer), but Trix had a history with this kind of excessive good fortune. It never lasted for long.

Lizinia loved the berries, as Trix suspected she would, and the root vegetables cooked nicely in the embers. The squirrel, the chipmunk, the groundhogs, and several other small animals joined Trix and Lizinia for the meal and slept by the warm fire. Before they fell asleep, Lizinia and Trix swapped stories under the stars. Lizinia told Trix some of her mother's and sister's escapades, though it had been so long she didn't recall much, nor did she want to. Trix regaled Lizinia with tales of life as a member of the legendary Woodcutter family and growing up in their towerhouse by the enchanted Wood.

"So your birthmother left you in the branches at the top of a tree for your papa to find? A baby? In the winter? That sounds dubious, even to me. I suppose your mother might have been able to climb a tree as well as you...but what if your papa hadn't noticed you way up there? Aren't those trees very old and terribly tall?"

Lizinia's questions were innocent, but the more she asked, the more the story Jack and Seven Woodcutter had told him all his life sounded a bit farfetched. "But Papa did notice me. Or, at least, I think he did. I don't know. I didn't even know who my birthmother was until a few months ago."

"But she was your foster mother's sister. If she knew her, why leave you in a tree? Why not just hand the baby over? Did your Mama hate her sister so much that she would have said no to her baby?"

Trix furrowed his brow and was forced to concede the issue. "Okay. Maybe it didn't really happen that way."

"Or maybe it did," Lizinia said kindly. "It sounds more like something's missing. Maybe you just don't have the whole story. The true story. Regardless, it is a good story."

That would have been just like Papa, making up a wonderful tale for Trix to tell instead of the tragic story of his abandonment. Perhaps that had been Papa's first gift to him.

"And you're traveling all this way to say farewell to a woman who didn't even know you? I may be kindhearted, Trix Woodcutter, but you're the purest soul I've ever known."

"I'm not so innocent," he said. "I've done terrible things."

Lizinia petted the fur of a mottled brown rabbit who had nuzzled into her stomach and fallen asleep there. "I have no doubt that your terrible things are still leagues better than most people's terrible things."

Trix thought about the terrible things that had been done to

Lizinia in her life. Even the "gift" her Papa Gatto had given her seemed as much of a burden as a blessing. The two of them had this much in common—they had both been cast out of their original birthfamilies in favor of households who loved and valued them. "We're both very lucky," said Trix. Lizinia gave a small hum in what Trix assumed was agreement.

"Trix," she asked, "do you believe in ghosts?"

"I believe in a lot of things," he answered honestly. "Some things exist only because we believe in them."

"So if I told you that I think I've been seeing the ghost of Papa Gatto now and again since we left the cottage, you would still be my friend?"

"My birthmother comes to me in my dreams, speaking riddles of the elements. She tells me I need to go see her," said Trix. "Are you still my friend?"

The whistle and wheeze of their little fire filled the space between sentences with cheerful song. "Of course you are my friend," Lizinia said finally.

"As you are mine," said Trix. He could almost hear her relief in the darkness.

"Papa says we need to take the rocky path," she whispered. "Not the one the deer told you to take."

"Okay," Trix answered sleepily. "I'll look at it in the morning."

By the light of day, however, the ghost cat's advice seemed positively ridiculous. The path Papa Gatto had suggested wasn't just "rocky," it was nigh impassable. Trix and Lizinia would have to scale a cliff wall down to a dry ravine cut deep into stone that looked as if it stretched all the way to the White Mountains. There would be no water, no food, no trees for shelter, and few animals to let them know where exactly they needed to climb out of the ravine and continue on to the Abbey.

The path the deer had suggested was lush and lined with giant flowers, which meant water sources and food and many other things Trix looked forward to discovering. There was nothing to discover in this ravine, other than how long Lizinia could walk on sharp rocks without her golden feet hurting. Trix didn't see Papa Gatto magicking *him* up a pair of golden boots any time soon.

Lizinia seemed up to the challenge—even excited by it—but Trix glowered. He'd been ordered around his whole life. By Mama and her magical powers of persuasion. By his absent, suddenly-attentive, and incredibly vague birthmother. And now thanks to an insubstantial cat he just so happened to adopt as a result of his own adventuring, he was being forced to endure pointless hardships. Was this another test he had to pass to prove his worthiness as Lizinia's companion?

Trix looked down the ravine once more and made a decision. "We're taking the garden path."

"But Papa Gatto—"

"I have taken Papa Gatto's advice under consideration. But if the garden path is good enough for the deer, it is good enough for us. We'll be fine."

Lizinia was not so easily convinced. She folded her arms over her chest. "Ask the tooth."

Trix rolled his eyes, but complied. He did not trust Papa Gatto as far as he could throw him (not that one could throw a ghost cat anywhere, no matter how hard one might wish it), but Wisdom's tooth had heretofore provided solid guidance. He pulled the necklace from beneath his shirt and held the tooth up before him.

"Dear Tooth"—he and Lizinia had decided that this was the best way to address such an important object—"do you think we should go down into the ravine?" Trix pivoted and pointed the tooth in the direction of the dense, green path. "Or should we go this way?"

The tooth did nothing.

"Try again," said Lizinia. "Maybe you're asking the wrong question."

"Or maybe it has no opinion," said Trix, but he tried again, for trying's sake. "We need to get to Rose Abbey, dear Tooth, and we'd like to get there soonish, so if you could please...look!" As Trix pointed toward the flower-lined path, the tooth glowed, ever so slightly. It was enough for Trix. "Well, that's decided. Let's go!"

Lizinia harrumphed but followed. Trix walked a little taller. *Take that, cat.*

The grass grew thick beneath Trix's bare feet as they traveled deeper into the lush greenery before them, so thick that the squirrel and chipmunk that accompanied them were nothing but eddies in the sea around them. The flowers, too, seemed to grow larger and more colorful the farther they went. Lizinia flitted excitedly from one to the next like a giant golden hummingbird. An amiable cloud of bees directed them to a honeysuckle vine from which they slaked their thirst on golden nectar. The dense canopy above shaded them from the blistering sun, and they danced and tumbled and laughed in a way that made the journey feel as if it took no time at all. Infinitely more pleasurable than a hike down a dusty ravine, for sure.

A brook ran through the colorful wilds, babbling and splashing with minnows as they made their journey. The sound was a delightful accompaniment to the sweet smells of the flowers, so powerful at times it was almost overwhelming. The squirrel and the chipmunk challenged their human companions to a game of chase. Trix and Lizinia accepted, tearing through the underbrush with gleeful abandon and howls of laughter.

It was for this reason that they did not immediately notice the rumble of the ground or the hum until it grew so loudly in their heads that they held their hands over their ears trying to stop the noise.

"WHAT IS THAT?" Lizinia yelled; Trix only knew because he read her lips. He shrugged, which seemed a silly gesture while both arms were raised. His heart pounded in his ears along with the buzzing—the feel of the earth moving beneath his feet sped his mind back to that earth-shattering, bone-breaking flood. It had been a miracle—several miracles—that he had survived it. He doubted Fate would be willing to roll the dice in his favor again.

Just as before, clouds covered the bright sun peeking through the colorful leaves and darkness filled the skies. But unlike before, there was no water falling from above or spouting up from below. The drone only grew louder.

And louder.

And louder.

She burst through the foliage and was upon him, her sleek black body toppling Trix with her tremendous weight and the speed of her attack. A multitude of thin, black, furred legs pawed at him, the claws at their ends catching on his clothes and drawing him close. The deafening hum came from her layers of rust-colored wings, and the wings of those in the army behind her. As she arched her strong body above him, all he could think was, *Not the stomach. Please, not the stomach.* Which was, of course, exactly where she struck.

There was no more buzzing in his head, though.

It had been drowned out by the sound of his own screams.

7

The Wasp Queen

rix needed a new word for pain.

Pain had been the pointed swords of the poison army in his stomach after consuming the bad stew that had enabled him to flee. Pain had been the cracking of his bones when the earth broke beneath him and chaos had reigned. Pain had been his heart breaking from the guilt of betraying a family who loved him.

The Wasp Queen's sting was something beyond pain. It was wildfire, exploding through his body and rendering every muscle inept, every mental command useless. He caught a glimpse of himself in the V of ebony eyes looming above him: his neck muscles tense, the screams tearing his mouth open so wide that he could see his back teeth.

There was a golden flash, and the crushing weight of the black monster left his chest. Small bundles of fur nudged at the side of his spasming body, first two, then more, pushing him through the thick grass and half-rolling him down a slight incline. He tasted the rich soil that found its way into his screaming mouth. A stone cut his cheek. His arms bent awkwardly beneath him. Trix felt nothing but the fire.

Suddenly he was in water—the stream they had been following?—too shallow for diving, but deep enough to drown. Something hard—a turtle?—held his head above the water so that Trix could continue breathing. And screaming. Minnows—tadpoles? Undines?—removed the tattered remnants of his shirt, swarmed his wound, sucked out the poison, washed it clean.

Somewhere, deep down, Trix wished to thank his wild friends for their assistance. The rest of him kept screaming, in tones of every register, until he had no more voice left to scream.

"You will not have him!"Lizinia's cry sounded muffled, or far away, or both.

"I do not know what armor you wear, human," buzzed the Wasp Queen, "but my warriors will crack you like a nut and suck out your insides all the same."

Lizinia would not have understood the Wasp Queen's rebuttal, but the intent to harm was certainly implied. If only he could get control of himself enough to help his new friend…if anything should happen to her, on top of everything else he had done to hurt people he loved recently, the guilt might very well kill him.

The small bit of bright gold Trix had glimpsed through the leaves was consumed in black in less than a moment. Trix's back arched and he cried out in hoarse frustration.

He needed to stand. He needed to find a weapon with which to beat those giant insects off Lizinia. He needed whatever idiot was screaming to stop so that he could think. Except that he was the idiot.

"Annoying, isn't it? The being helpless part?"

Trix turned his head enough to see Tesera perched on a rock in the stream above him. Her long hair fell in cinnamon waves down to where her blue-green dress of water lilies pooled in the stream about her. Dragonflies lit in a row like a tiara on her brow. A small, colorful tree frog perched upon the large ring on her finger.

It was just as well that his body could not summon the words to answer her. He did not know whether to address the vision of his birthmother with kindness, curiosity, or anger. Constant, head-splintering squeals seemed as good a response as any.

"Relax, my boy—for all that you are hardly a boy anymore. Let the waters work their magic."

Trix tried to do as the vision bade, managing only to close his eyes. Soon after, he managed to clamp his jaw shut, reveling in the silent skull now free from his screams. He heard commotion in the brush up the hill. Trix hoped it was Lizinia, managing to hold her own.

"She's a scrapper, your golden girl," Tesera confirmed. "I like her. Granted, you probably should have heeded her godfather's advice."

Trix was afraid to open his mouth again, for fear that the shrieking would resume.

"I never listened to anyone either. You're much like me in that way." She smiled beatifically. "Oh, there is so much you should know."

Trix did not want to know. He did not want to hear that he was like his birthmother in any way. She had abandoned him, willfully forfeiting any part in his life. Trix never wanted to abandon anyone, be they animal or human or anything else. His one true desire was to be helpful to those he loved, despite the sometimes disastrous outcomes of his actions. Indeed, this whole journey was at his birthmother's request, to help *her*. Why must she plague him so? If he wanted to be pestered, he could get that from his sisters. Right now, he just wanted the use of his arms and legs so that he could help Lizinia.

"You should be able to walk now. But go quickly. There is still yet so far to go."

Trix flipped over in the shallow stream, braced his hands and knees upon the silty bottom, and slowly rose to standing. For a moment, he spotted a strange reflection beneath him. Was that his face?

With a flick of her ghosty hand, Tesera tossed the frog into the water, distorting the image. "I said '*quickly*.' Get on with you!"

The moment Tesera disappeared, something washed over Trix—*inside* Trix—that took all the pain away. He nodded a thanks to the Water Gods before speeding up the hill. Neither the squirrel nor the chipmunk were fast enough to halt his progress, but a sparrow managed to fly into his face before he reached the clearing where Lizinia fought her attackers. Peeking through the thick leaves, Trix assessed the situation.

The swarm of wasps was thick. There were dozens—maybe a hundred—of them, blotting out the sun and casting the small clearing in shade. Each were larger than any wasp he'd ever encountered, but none were as big as their queen. Lizinia swatted at her attackers with a broken tree branch. Try as they might, the wasps' stingers slid off her skin as they would have any suit of armor.

Trix closed his eyes and summoned good thoughts about cats. *Thank you, Papa Gatto!*

His own meager weapon would no doubt be futile against an army this massive, so he decided to save the lingworm's dagger for a more opportune moment. If he was calculating enough, he might be able to get a drop on the queen. If he could find a way to control her, it was possible he could control her minions as well.

As if reading his mind, the chipmunk and squirrel scurried up the tree beside him. With a nod, Trix followed them. *Thanks, friends.*

In a moment, he was high above the fray—still beneath the cloud cover of wasps, but over Lizinia's head and the wasp queen's as she shouted orders. "Steel! Thisbe! There are far more of us than there are of her. Why can no one stop her?"

"She's slippery," a female warrior said.

"That's not skin," buzzed another female. "Our stingers cannot penetrate."

"Then stop trying to kill her," yelled the queen. "Just *stop* her!"

Five wasp-warriors flew at Lizinia the moment the queen made her command, toppling the golden girl and overpowering her.

"*NO!*" Lizinia cried.

The Wasp Queen let out a wicked laugh.

Trix leapt.

Holding onto the giant Wasp Queen was a bit like riding a wild boar for the first time. She bucked and thrashed beneath him and his hands scrabbled to find purchase anywhere on her ebony carapace. He grasped her antennae and mandibles alternately, maneuvering around enough to wrap his legs around her scrawny neck and lock them there. He drew his golden dagger and pressed it into the base of her head.

"Order them to let her go!" he commanded in a ruined voice that sounded little like his own.

Trix gave the queen a moment to recognize the realness of his threat. Her body quieted beneath him, bowing under his weight until her forehead almost touched the ground. Trix could make out Lizinia's golden hand beneath the press of the wasps. It lay there still, unmoving.

"Let her go," the queen said reluctantly.

"But your majesty," said one wasp. Her blue-black shell seemed to absorb all the light around it.

A second wasp clouted the first with a long claw. "You heard Queen Sphex. Step off, Thisbe."

The wasps did as asked, moving away from Lizinia's body…but not far.

"Lizinia!" Trix called, but she did not move. "Lizinia!"

"Tsk, tsk." Queen Sphex clicked her mandibles reproachfully.

"What now, youngling? Do you risk my release to see to the health of your maiden fair? Choose quickly."

"Why does everyone keep telling me to hurry up?" Trix bellowed. "Can't I just take a moment to think? Please?"

"But of course, human-child," Queen Sphex crooned. "Take all the time that you need. I only urge you to make your decision in the next few moments, before the numbness of my sting sets in."

Trix's left foot had already turned from pins and needles to stone. He lost his hold on the Wasp Queen's neck and tumbled to the ground beneath her. He managed to keep the golden dagger in his grasp, but he wasn't sure how much longer he would have the use of his arm.

She bent over him as she had when she'd attacked him, and once again he saw his distorted face multiplied in her myriad eyes. "Unlike my ruthless warriors, I do not sting to kill," said the queen. "I sting to preserve. You will stay alive, a nice warm shell to protect the eggs I lay inside you. Together, we will breed a new army. A strong army." She stepped over his body and loomed above Lizinia. "And when we figure out how to crack the shell of your golden friend—and I assure you, we will—she will be the birthplace of our new queen." With that, the Wasp Queen threw her head back and laughed mightily.

It was Trix's last chance. He had to fling his dagger straight at the Wasp Queen's head, and his aim had to be true. But which eye would be the most vulnerable? He decided to aim for the larger one on the Wasp Queen's right side, hoping that if his arm was significantly hampered by the paralytic sting that he'd still hit something vital enough to stop her…and, with luck, her army as well. Trix clenched his stomach muscles in preparation, summoning all of his strength into his throwing arm and…nothing happened.

Worried that he had lost that limb—and subsequently his fruitful young life—to the Wasp Queen, Trix glanced up at the hand that held the dagger. It was fixed to the ground, completely covered in spider webs. There was no escape—his arm may as well have been encased in glue. But the lingworm had said the golden dagger would cut through anything, so Trix wriggled the blade about inside the trap just the same.

"Sorry it took us so long to get here," a small voice said in his ear. "But we have arrived. Don't move. We've got this." The spider's legs were but a tickle on his skin as she crawled down the side of his jaw and neck to stand bravely on Trix's bare chest. There was a shell-like structure on her back that looked as if it had been covered in bird droppings. "AY! SHE-WITCH!" she cried. "LET OUR FRIENDS GO!"

Trix was taken aback at the powerful voice that emanated from a body no bigger than Wisdom's Tooth.

The Wasp Queen stopped mid-cackle to search for the source of the barked order. When she found it she chuckled again, this time in low, evil tones. The buzzing hum of her army started again, vibrating Trix to his core. Their wings stirred up a whirlwind, tossing the leaves and grass about in a malicious tumult. "Brave words, little one," Queen Sphex said with great condescension, "but I believe I will be keeping my prey this evening, if you don't mind."

"It's not my mind you need to worry about," the little spider said curtly.

For a moment—the smallest, briefest moment—the Wasp Queen looked...worried? Surprised? Not frightened, certainly...

There was a rustle in the brush. A shadowy figure emerged from the leaves, a furry lump only half as tall as Queen Sphex, but easily twice as wide, and several times again after that had all eight of its legs not been bent quite close to its body. The enormous spider bowed to the Wasp Queen.

The Wasp Queen did not bow. If anything, she stood taller, head held high, layers of wings beating madly.

"With respect," said the spider. His voice was as deep as the sea and old as the mountains.

The Wasp Queen said nothing, only hummed, louder and louder. In an instant the spider had enveloped the Wasp Queen, jumping on her much in the same way she had jumped on Trix.

Trix tilted his head down to the small spider perched patiently on his chest. "I did not see that coming."

The spider shrugged in the wholly satisfying way that only a creature with eight legs can shrug. "I warned her. Now, have you cut yourself free yet? We should see to your friend."

Queen Sphex wrestled out from the Great Spider's clutches and reared her stinger high, but just as she thought she'd won, the spider flipped her over and trapped her inside the prison of his long legs once more. Trix *had* just about hacked through the sticky web trap with his blade, but his mind was on other things. Great Spider or not, they were still outnumbered, and by a lot. "What about the rest of her army?"

"My family will see to them," the spider said nonchalantly, as if a warring faction of enormous wasps visited themselves upon them every other day. Trix tilted his head back to see the forest around them shifting…*moving*…a dark layer beneath the leaves and the grass, separate from the ground. Spindly-legged creatures great and small and of varying colors silently spilled over the earth and up the trees like oil spreading across water. In no time at all, Queen Sphex's army was surrounded. Strands of sticky web shot out from the surrounding trees. Spiders with gossamer nets like Needa's dropped from the sky in legion. Tiny red spiders slid up the wasp-warriors' legs, and larger furred spiders—though not quite so large as the Great Spider—made quick work of binding the wasps who were not fast enough.

Trix freed his hand and sat up, slapping the life back into his legs. The spider that had situated herself on his chest moved to his shoulder, attacking any wasp that came near them with a pasty globule of flying webmatter. Trix managed to sit up, but his lower limbs still wouldn't respond. Tucking the lingworm's dagger back into his belt, he used his upper body to drag himself across the clearing to where Lizinia lay. He'd thought the task would be harder than it was—had the Queen's poison somehow made him stronger?—thankfully, he was at her side in almost no time at all.

"Lizinia." Trix pulled himself up next to her, situating his legs beneath him so that he was once again in a sitting position. His knees had begun to tingle in a warm, unpleasant way, but he took that as a good sign.

"Lizinia," he called again. He laid a hand on her arm. It was cold to the touch. He tried not to be worried—when he had held her hands before they had been warm, but it was sunny and metal warmed in the sun. In this shade, it was reasonable to believe that she would be cold to the touch for some other reason than...

"Lizinia!" Trix said more urgently. Shaking her was like trying to shake a statue. Around them, the cacophony of warring wildlife carried on. The birds had joined in to fly in the faces of the wasps and the squirrels and chipmunks barreled heedlessly into the fray, but the rest of the forest creatures kept their distance. In a battle between two such deadly enemies, no one wanted to be an accidental casualty...or a post-skirmish snack.

"Is it over?" he heard her say, and he breathed a sigh of relief.

"Not quite," he admitted. "But I suspect it will be soon."

She had not yet turned to face him. "I couldn't beat them," she said. "I watched them kill you, and I tried my best to avenge you, but there were too many."

"Lizinia, I'm not dead. A bit worse for the wear maybe, and I'm not sure when my legs will function properly again, but...*oof.*" Like golden lightning she'd sat up and thrown her arms around him in another enthusiastic, Friday-style embrace.

"I was so scared," she said into his neck.

"You needn't have been," he said reassuringly. "I saw you fighting those wasps. You were amazing! And your gold protected you—that's a handy thing."

"I was scared for *you,*" she clarified. "Don't die again. Please."

"I'll do my best, but I'll have a much better chance if you don't squeeze me to bits first."

She released him, pulling back to survey the damage. She looked him over from head to toe, tilting her head in that same broken-clockwork way she had before. Trix had only caught a glimpse of his distorted self in the running stream and the eyes of the Wasp Queen—he couldn't imagine what a mess he'd become. His shirt was gone—not that it mattered, now that he was covered in mud, grass, and river filth from head to toe. There was still webmatter stuck to his hand, and the hilt of the lingworm's dagger, and he was pretty sure there was some in his hair. Among other things. "Is it really all that bad?" he asked finally.

"Why don't your legs work?"

"The sting was poison, but not deadly. Queen Sphex never intended to kill me."

"Sphex? That was her name? Charming," said Lizinia, in a tone that meant she'd found nothing charming at all about the Wasp Queen. "She was going to take you back to her nest and eat you, I suppose."

"Probably," Trix agreed.

"Why are you lying to your friend?" asked the spider on his shoulder.

Trix was ashamed to admit he'd forgotten that his small, hard-shelled champion was still there. "Because she doesn't need to know."

"What don't I need to know?" asked Lizinia.

Trix sighed. His sisters had caught him in this trap a thousand times before. He really should have been better at it. "Sphex wasn't going to eat me. She was going to lay her eggs inside my body while I was still alive to protect them. And she intended the same for you, too."

Lizinia wrinkled her nose—the golden skin between her eyes actually wrinkled. "He's right," she said to the spider. "I didn't need to know."

The spider laughed, which needed little translation.

"I'm Lizinia, by the way. Thank you and your friends for coming to our rescue."

"I am Bala." The spider bowed. "And you are welcome, though my family came only to fulfill our obligation."

"Her name is Bala," Trix said to Lizinia. "What obligation?" he asked the spider.

There was no time to answer. The Wasp Queen had escaped the Great Spider's clutches once again, but instead of returning his attack, she flew straight at Trix and Lizinia.

"*MIIIIIIIIIIIIINE!*"

Lizinia's arm flew forward and hit the Wasp Queen square in the nose. At the same time, Bala let another glob of her sticky webstuff fly, hitting the queen in two of her eyes. The queen roared mightily and headed for the skies, her layers of wings beating the grass around them into a frenzy. The rest of her army—the ones not still actively engaged in battle—followed angrily in her wake, disappearing into the rest of the dark clouds that had moved in overhead.

"Thank you," Trix breathed. When he found his battered voice again, he spoke to the clearing at large. "Thank you, all."

The Great Spider came forward. Trix half expected him to be a lumbering brute for all his girth, but this was not the case. The Great Spider moved with ease and silence, the black and gray hairs on his legs waving like a dance. He stopped before Trix and Lizinia and tilted his head down, eyes cast to the ground. Awkward as it was, Trix did the same, bowing as low as he could from his sitting position.

"With respect," Bala said formally, "may I present Bofu, King of Spiders."

"I am honored," said Trix. "King Bofu, I am Trix Woodcutter. This is my friend Lizinia." Lizinia had caught either Trix's body language or the hint in his address, for she had bowed her head as well. "We thank you most kindly for your assistance. You have saved our lives."

"Much obliged," the king said. His voice was slow and deep and soft. "My apologies for the delay in reaching you. Our home is in the dry valley to the west. We venture here only on hunting days. We find the area…less than hospitable due to its inhabitants."

Trix felt Lizinia pinch his arm, hard. That valley to the west was where Papa Gatto had tried to send them in the first place and Trix hadn't listened. Just like Tesera.

"But why in the world would you feel obligated to help me?" The words fell out of Trix all at once and then he remembered he was talking to the King of Spiders. "Your Majesty," he added quickly.

"We are calling it The Catastrophe of Arilland," said King Bofu.

"You saved the life of a young mother as well as the lives of her children. This part of our family would not be with us today if not for you. It was our honor to come to your aid." The Great Spider's words dripped with the wisdom of his years.

"You honor me," said Trix.

"And me," Lizinia added. She could not know what the King of Spiders had said, though she seemed adept at picking up clues from only one side of a conversation.

Trix bowed again. "I shall consider the debt repaid, but truly, it was a kindness I would have performed for anyone in that situation. To not do so would have been inhuman."

The Great Spider chuckled a deep, whuffling laugh, and the fine hairs on his legs shifted like autumn hay in the wind. "With respect," said the king, "there are only two of you. Needa has hundreds of children. It is possible this 'debt' will never be repaid in our lifetime."

Trix couldn't help but smile. "Good point."

"Nor are you so human yourself, are you, Boy Who Talks to Animals?"

Trix bowed his head once again, but this time not in reverence. "No. I suppose not entirely."

"Then your kindness cannot be attributed solely to your humanity. But it can be credited solely to you. You are a kind boy, Trix Woodcutter, and we are honored to have you in this family."

"Again, the honor is mine," said Trix. He hated that he could not stand and bow in respect to this great king, who had summoned his family to save Trix's sorry carcass. Mama would have been so disappointed. Awkwardly, Trix tried once more to shift his weight into his arms.

"Here, I will help you," Lizinia said as she got to her feet.

"We will help you," said King Bofu, almost at the same time. "Our family will accompany you to the stream's end. From there you and your companion may make your way north unhindered. We will see to it."

Trix translated for Lizinia, who thanked the spiders politely. She helped Trix rise and positioned him on the back of a short, flat, wine-dark spider with beautiful patterns on its body and legs. Slowly they moved through the thick grass.

Lizinia walked closely beside Trix, helping him should he begin to slide off the spider's back. Which he did. Almost. A few times. "The flowers don't seem quite as beautiful as when we first took this path, do they?" she asked quietly.

"They don't," said Trix. "I'm sorry I didn't listen to Papa Gatto."

"Me too," she said with a grin.

"Why do you suppose Wisdom's Tooth brought us this way?"

Lizinia shrugged. "It did hesitate—perhaps it was weighting the chance of wasps against the certainty of spiders. Somehow, Papa Gatto must have known the spiders would welcome you."

"Still. I'm sorry I got you into this mess."

"Stop beating yourself up," she said. "It was scary, yes, but I'm glad to have met your friends. Of course, Papa Gatto may not be so forgiving."

"No, I imagine not." Papa Gatto was like Mama Woodcutter in

so many ways. Lizinia, on the other hand, was like all of his sisters, and none of them. And the King of Spiders had called him family. Perhaps he was not so alone in the world after all.

"You know," said Lizinia, "I vaguely remember that I didn't care for spiders at some point, long ago, though for the life of me I can't remember why. They are truly lovely creatures."

"It's good of you to say that," said Trix. "Because they've adopted me."

"Have they?" Lizinia said with great condescension. "Did they make you a prince as well? Will you be growing a few more limbs now, to match the rest of you?"

Trix thought her prince joke as good as any his sisters might make, but before he could ask about the second half of what she'd said, a screeching, buzzing whirlwind flew out of the dense foliage.

"*DEATH TO THE HUMANS!*"

8

The Broken Mirror

rix shoved Lizinia with all his might, getting her as far away as he could before the screeching black body slammed into him. He tumbled off the spider onto the unforgiving ground, thanking his good fortune for what numbness still remained within him and cursing his luck for what had already gone. Once more, he found himself pressed into the dirt by another angry wasp. Though the attack had been a surprise, he found himself less afraid this time. He could tell by the shade of her carapace and the slant of the eyes in her smaller head that his attacker was not the queen.

"Thisbe?" he choked out when he found his breath.

"*DO NOT PRETEND TO KNOW ME, FOUL HUMAN. INSTEAD, KNOW MY WRATH.*"

The blue-black wasp reared up to impale him with her stinger, only to be met by an avalanche of spiders and webbing. They made quick work of wrapping her from head to stinger. Struggle as she might, there was no escape.

"She's alone," a tiger-striped spider called from his vantage point in the trees.

King Bofu slunk forward and bent over their bundled foe. "What would your queen say if she knew you were here against her orders?"

Thisbe's voice was muffled by webstuff, but she managed to make herself understood. "She would commend me for my brave sacrifice."

"Or exile you for insanity," said Bala.

"Perhaps it is a blessing, then, that you will never know," said King Bofu. "Bring her along. She will make a lovely present for my wife."

"What will they do with her?" Lizinia asked as she helped Trix back up onto the back of the spider he'd been riding. It was slightly less awkward this time, as the feeling in his legs had transformed from a vague sparkly numbness to a shadow of the fire he'd felt when he'd first been stung. More painful, but more useable.

Trix tried to think of a way to put it kindly. "She will be presented to the queen."

"Ah," said Lizinia. And then, as she understood, "*Ah.*"

"I do not envy Thisbe her fate," said Trix.

"Says the half-paralyzed boy currently using a spider for legs. I don't imagine anyone would envy *you* after all you've been through recently. You are a stubborn thing, Trix Woodcutter."

"I get that from my mother," he said lowly. "Or so I've heard."

"Was she unbreakable, too, your mother?"

Lizinia knew that she was not, since they were traveling to her sepulcher, but she had asked the question so he must answer. "No," he said. "I suppose that part is all me."

"I suppose it is."

As promised, the spiders delivered them safely to the stream's end. The lush, flowering greenery gave way to a forest of trees—nothing like the old, dense Enchanted Wood Trix knew from home, but the place felt familiar enough to him all the same. He and Lizinia both thanked the spiders profusely, bowing so many times as they bid their farewells that Trix thought his head might just fall off his poor body.

The spiders had set him up beneath a sturdy oak tree. Though all his limbs were now functioning properly, he still felt as worn out as one of Mama's old dishrags. Lizinia had offered to collect firewood, but Trix had no firestone or wisplight to make it burn. Nor had they encountered any more helpful animal friends along their travels, most animals having sense enough to stay away from a king's legion of spiders. He took the risk of sending her off to hunt down what berries and other edibles she could—he'd just sort through them all upon her return to make sure she hadn't stumbled upon anything dangerous.

In her absence, he took stock of the situation. By the spiders' reckoning, they were now back on track and would reach Rose Abbey within the next day. His considerable lack of shirt and shoes made him somewhat less than presentable—Mama would be mortified if she knew he'd be calling on one of his many aunts in such a state. He might have asked the spiders to pause at stream's end for a bath, but it seemed a frivolous request, requiring more energy than he suspected he had at the moment.

He lifted Wisdom's Tooth from its place on his weary, dirty chest, thankful that Lizinia'd had the presence of mind to fashion the necklace for him. Everything in his shirt pockets was gone now, but they still had the bag of apples, both golden and flesh. The first would only serve as sustenance if they happened upon an inn or waystation in this forest—the latter would have to serve in the meantime, no matter how battered and bruised the fruit might be for all its unintended adventuring.

For some reason, Wisdom's Tooth seemed smaller than it had when he'd rescued it from the surf at his feet. But then, it was hard to believe that he'd encountered the lingworm only a few days ago.

He hoped the abbess would pity them enough to offer a bed for the night. Trix missed sleeping in a real bed.

"Papa Gatto said we should stay here until daybreak." Lizinia dropped the contents of her skirt at Trix's feet—a variety of roots and berries and mushrooms and moss...very little of it edible.

"Just as well," he said. His voice was still raspy from screaming, and he seemed to have lost all control over his tonal register. "I've fallen asleep three times since you've been gone."

"I don't mind. It's been a long day. You deserve your rest." She held up her treasures. "Do you want to eat something first?"

"You're welcome to the blackberries," he croaked. "Beyond

that I'm afraid it will have to be apples."

Lizinia sighed and nodded, plopping down cross-legged beside him. "You sleep. I'll keep watch."

"Rest if you can," Trix said with a yawn. "The spiders said they would keep us safe. And you never know what adventures tomorrow will bring."

"With you, Trix Woodcutter, that is a real threat."

Trix wanted to laugh in earnest at her jest, but the stress of the day was settling into his weary, tortured bones. He gathered the dry leaves at the base of the tree, curling up and making himself as comfortable as he could. It was a shame they didn't have a fire, but it was a pleasant enough evening. There was only the slightest chill in the crisp autumn night, but only because he wasn't fully clothed. Just as long as...

And then he heard it: three plinks in quick succession from somewhere in Lizinia's direction, followed by three more.

"Trix? I think it's—"

The sky opened up.

"—raining."

❧

Earth breaks.
Fire breathes.
Waters bless.
Fly to me, my son.

Trix woke to Lizinia staring at him. She still wore her dark hooded cloak, but her golden dress was hidden beneath the plain white robes of an acolyte.

Trix sat straight up. Blankets and sheets fell away from his body. *Blankets. Sheets. Bed.* He was in a bed.

"Where am I?" Trix put a hand around his throat. His wrecked voice was still hollow. "What happened?"

Lizinia handed him a goblet of water. "I fell asleep under the tree in the rain and woke up the next morning, but you did not. You were cold and shaking and I was...worried. So I carried you."

"You carried me all the way to the abbey?" Lizinia was obviously far stronger than he'd realized.

"There didn't seem to be much choice."

"You could have waited."

"I've waited for most of my life. I believe I am tired of waiting. Besides, the animals helped. They all knew the way. There are many animals here. And some beautiful gardens." Trix could tell from Lizinia's humor that she, too, was adequately rested.

"All those diversions and you decided you'd rather spend your time staring at me?"

She shrugged. "I haven't gotten tired of looking at you yet."

"Thank you...I guess." While it was true that the animals constantly sought him out, Trix wasn't used to any *person* being so fascinated with him. Even in a family as special as the Woodcutters, he was just one of many. Because of their closeness in age, he and Sunday had always been thick as thieves, but even she had never been...enraptured...simply by his presence. He wasn't sure how he felt about it.

He did, however, feel cleaner, warmer, and well-rested. He was on a cot in some sort of bedchamber, covered in hand-stitched quilts and—blessedly—fully clothed in a fresh shirt and trousers. He put a hand to his chest and was relieved to find Wisdom's Tooth still with him.

"Did you know they separated the men's rooms and the women's rooms here?" Lizinia asked him. "It seems that a great deal more women than men visit this place, so the women's rooms are much larger and grander."

"Why didn't you stay there? Do some exploring?"

Lizinia averted her eyes. "I find I don't care for being alone."

Trix tried to imagine the days, months, years that Lizinia had been alone in the house of cats after the colony had perished. So much loss…it was no wonder she craved companionship now that she had escaped her prison. "I'm surprised they let you in the men's wing, then. Places like this don't normally do that."

"Oh, they didn't want to," Lizinia admitted. "Your aunt put up quite a fuss. But in the end she told me I was….very persuasive."

If the abbess was anything like Mama, Trix imagined that exchange had been quite a scene. He was almost sorry to have missed it. More immediately, his stomach was sorry to have missed whatever dinner had been served during his unexpected slumber. It caught the scent of food and growled with a tremendous ferocity that made Lizinia laugh.

"You may not always want to eat, Trix Woodcutter, but your stomach certainly does."

"I'm a growing boy," he said. It's what he always said.

"You don't think you've grown enough already? Goodness." Even as she teased him, she crossed the room to retrieve a covered silver plate. "The abbess sent this for you, when you awoke. I am to tell you that the deer was shot with blessed arrows, and that its soul was honored in the Hall of the Mother Goddess. She said it would matter to you."

"It does, thank you," said Trix. When possible, Trix did not partake of the meat of his animal brethren, though he had done so when times were tight, food was scarce, and needs must. Knowing that this meal had been blessed by the Earth Goddess, that the animal had not suffered unduly and had gone on to serve his purpose in the cycle of life made Trix's heart easier about sating the mad hunger within him. Servants of this goddess saw to the needs of all earth's creatures, be they human, fey, animal or otherwise. Under this roof, Trix could be assured that none of this friend's sacrifice had been wasted, and that the balance of the world had been maintained.

Which was good, as he had witnessed too much unbalancing of the world lately.

"The abbess said she was your mother's sister," said Lizinia. "Both of your mothers."

Trix nodded while shoving bread and meat and cheese alternately into his gob. If Lizinia minded his lack of social graces, she thankfully made no mention of it. "My grandmother had seven children, all girls."

"Goodness," said Lizinia. "You all have such great, large families. Peppina was difficult enough—I can't bear to think of five more like her."

"It's a challenge and not without adventure. Much like living with cats, I imagine." Trix reached down for more food and found that he'd already cleaned his plate. Lizinia handed him the rest of the loaf of bread from the table, but left the pretty bowl of apples there untouched. He might be sad not to see another apple again, but that wouldn't be for a very long time.

"My birthmother was the fourth born," he told her. "The abbess was the sixth. Mama Woodcutter was the seventh." Trix considered his own gaggle of sisters. Thursday had been the fourth born and she'd run away to become a pirate queen, much as Tesera had run off to become an actress. Saturday was sixth in line and Sunday was the seventh. Despite all her wishes to the contrary, Trix could see Sunday taking after Mama, given time. For the life of him, though, Trix could not imagine Saturday in the role of abbess. Saturday was far more likely to fight a god—or *be* a god— than she was to spend her life worshipping one.

Once again, there was suddenly nothing left to eat. Trix sighed. "Speaking of my aunt, I suppose I better clean up and go see her." His birthmother's chant echoed in his ears: *Earth breaks; fire breathes; waters bless. Fly to me, my son.* "And get the rest of this over with," he added. He walked over to the full-length mirror, but turned back to Lizinia before examining himself in it. "You don't have to do that, you know. The acolytes will take care of it."

Lizinia fluffed up his pillow and straightened his rumpled bedsheets with a practiced hand. "This is something I know how to do," she said. "Let me do it."

So he did. Trix shrugged and turned back to the mirror. Not that it was much help, as it seemed to be a Lying Mirror. The face inside its worn, gilded frame was definitely not his own. He lifted a hand and waved. The young man in the mirror waved back. Trix poked at the mirror—it seemed solid enough. Then he poked at his face. The image also poked his face.

"This mirror is broken," he said.

Lizinia pulled the top sheet of the bed tight and walked over to stand behind him. "No, it's not."

Trix pointed at the image before him. "Then who is *THAT?*" His shattered voice broke on the last word.

Lizinia surveyed the young man in the mirror from head to toe. Matter-of-factly she stated, "It's you."

Trix studied the image again in horror and fascination. The man in the mirror had his wild cinnamon hair, dark brows and dark eyes, but he was taller than Trix had ever been, and easily twice as wide. Not quite so broad in the shoulders as his woodcutter brother Peter, but still far more substantial than the boy who'd run from the towerhouse. Trix prodded his arms through the sleeves of his new shirt. There were *muscles* there, not spindly, breakable skin and bones. No wonder he'd been able to pull himself up so easily after that terrible wasp's sting. Well, there'd certainly be no more shimmying into mole holes and rabbit warrens for him...but when had this happened?

And then his attention shifted back to Lizinia's reflection, staring at him again with that cockeyed, clockwork tilt of her head...the same look she'd been giving him since he'd left the cats' house…

Trix's face flushed with fury and he clenched his fists. He could feel the muscles of his chest and stomach tense in response. "Papa Gatto," he said deeply. He suspected the voice he'd lost during the fight with the wasps would never be his voice again, either.

Lizinia's eyebrows raised at his surprise. "I thought you knew."

Trix turned away from the distracting mirror and closed his eyes. He thought back to all of the odd comments Lizinia had made about him having grown or changed…of the times in the past few days when he'd half-caught a glimpse of his strange reflection but been too busy to study it at length…

"I assumed it was his gift to you, like my gold, or Peppina's humiliation."

Trix slipped back into the chair, leaned over the table and put his head in hands that now seemed overly large and foreign. "What kind of gift was *this*?" But as soon as he asked it, he knew. Papa Gatto did not trust his golden goddaughter with a scrawny scamp who survived by using his wits and his animal friends. Trix knew his fey blood would always keep him looking younger than his years. Somehow, Papa Gatto had forced Trix's body to catch up.

And that was it. Even more than looking older—being older— Trix was bothered by the fact that the image in the mirror looked…human. He'd had all of his life to come to terms with being fey. He was fine with the idea of being part animal. But he was not prepared to be human.

A golden hand slipped into his, and golden fingers curled around his own. "One person walked inside that house, and one person walked out," said Lizinia. "I was there, so I would know. It was the same person. And that person was Trix Woodcutter."

Trix raised his head and studied Lizinia in earnest. She was all too familiar with what it was like to survive a cat's "blessing", to come out on the other side completely changed on the outside, while still completely the same on the inside.

"What color was your hair?" he asked her.

"Black."

"Do you miss it?"

Lizinia ran the fingers that weren't holding Trix's through her golden tresses. The strands caught the lamplight. Trix had watched Sunday spin wool into gold once, but the result wasn't as fine as Lizinia's hair was now. "Sometimes I miss it," she said finally. "But I think I like who I am now." She squeezed his hand. "And I like who *you* are. You will too. You'll see."

She was probably right, but even still... "It will take some getting used to."

Lizinia smiled. "Just think of it as another adventure."

9

The Ghost of Rose Abbey

ad he still been inside a boy's body, Trix would have skipped merrily through the gardens of Rose Abbey. They were beautiful and full of colorful blossoms, even this far north and this late in the year. It was a proud foliage that deserved to be skipped through, but this man's body—now that he was aware of it—felt heavy and awkward. He'd bumped into two doorways following Lizinia out to the courtyard. He was thankful for the abbey's high ceilings, or he might have banged his noggin on those as well.

Scattered throughout the gardens of greenery and late-blooming flowers were various topiaries and groups of white-robed acolytes. The topiaries fascinated Trix. Conversely, the acolytes seemed to be fascinated by him. Some even giggled in his wake as they passed. He knew why, of course—silly young girls had often giggled when Peter walked by. Some of them had even made fools of themselves by falling directly into Peter's path, or pretending to faint so he would catch them in arms that chopped down trees all day and would one day be large enough to rival Papa's.

Thankfully, the acolytes here limited themselves to smiles and giggles. Trix made sure to keep Lizinia's pace, in case he needed her protection.

The gardens also housed various feeding troughs and sanctuaries for whatever beast happened to be passing through. Interspersed with the sanctuaries were acolytes communing—non-verbally—with the various groups of animals. For the first time, he realized just how exceptional it was, this gift he'd had all his life.

And then, suddenly, the shadow of the great chapel loomed above them. They were here. Trix took a deep breath. There was only so long he could put off the inevitable. Together, he and Lizinia pushed open the carved wooden doors.

The chapel itself was filled with archways, separating the smaller rooms from the larger area of worship. The late afternoon sun shone through the many-colored windows of the entranceway and splattered the floor with rainbows. The rest of the chapel was dark, however, and almost entirely made of wood. Stained benches like tree stumps rose up from the ground. A massive phalanx of grand beasts stood along the walls, watching over the room with protective eyes. Trix bowed to them each in turn: the Bear, the Cat, the Wolf, and the Serpent. Embracing the altar were more enormous and exquisitely detailed woodcarvings, the crowning glory of which was the Great Hart.

Behind the altar, stood the abbess. She waited patiently for Trix to pay his respects to the Earth Goddess before addressing him. Her wine-red robes hung gracefully about her tall, thick body, emphasizing what little auburn remained in her mostly silver hair.

"Trix Woodcutter." She stepped down from the altar and approached him, holding him at arm's length and studying him from head to toe. Mama often did the same, looking for scrapes and bruises after he'd come home covered in half the Wood. "It seems you've grown," she said, as if she had not seen him for some time, though Trix doubted she had ever laid eyes on him at all.

Trix was unsure how much of their adventure Lizinia had already shared with the abbess. "Most of it is a recent acquisition. I'm still getting used to it."

"Even late bloomers must bloom sometime," said his aunt. "Take that from a woman who named herself after a flower."

"Yes, Your Excellence."

"Goodness." She waved her hand at him. "None of that nonsense. Aunt, Auntie Rose, Rose Red…any of those will do nicely. I hear you've come to see your birthmother. Though why you've shown up at my door without any other family is a story whose details your lovely companion here doesn't seem to know."

"Tesera herself told me to come," he admitted. "I've been having visions of her for some time now. She's very persistent."

"Is that so." Rose Red tapped the ring of keys on her belt absentmindedly. "That does sound like my sister."

"And if I'd so much as hinted to Mama about my intention to

leave, she would have forbade it. Nor did I want to ask her and risk the chance that she might say no."

"That sounds like a sister of mine, too." Rose Red gave a half-smile, but it fell again quickly. "I should probably reprimand you, child, or at the very least give you a stern talking-to, but I'm afraid my heart just isn't in it right now. You've come all this way; I'll let you pay your respects."

She took Trix by the hand and led them into a small, gray room behind the altar. Where the chapel had been wood, this sacristy was stone. Thin shafts of light split the darkness like golden daggers in an apple, the beams falling upon two low oaken tables in the center of the room. A woman lay still upon each of them.

Trix released his aunt's hand. The family resemblance between the two supine women was unmistakable. Each wore a simple white dress and their bodies had been surrounded by flowers. Trix blinked his eyes rapidly as the smell of them rose up to meet him. It was a sad thing being in this place. It would have been a sad thing even if these women had been perfect strangers.

Which they almost were.

Slow step by slow step, Trix moved between the tables. The room was so quiet that Trix heard nothing but his breath and his heartbeat and the shuffle of his feet against the stones. The woman farthest from the door had silvery silken hair. There was kindness in her face and strength in the hands that clasped the lily at her breast. His own sister Friday possessed such kindness—this woman looked as Friday might look one day, when Lord Death's Angels came for her. Trix surmised that this must be *Teresa*, master seamstress and the third Mouton sister. Rose Red had not mentioned her passing to him.

Trix turned back to the abbess in confusion—she and Lizinia still waited politely by the entrance to the sacristy. He opened his mouth to speak, but the sight of his birthmother transfixed him.

Tesera's long, chestnut locks had been laid in graceful waves down her sides and sprinkled with vervain and bettany. There were laugh lines in the corners of her eyes and around her pale pink lips that, even in death, seem slightly curved upward as if at any moment she would break into a smile. Gently, he placed a hand atop the ones folded upon her gossamer dress. Her skin did not feel as cold as he imagined. Lizinia's hands were far colder when not warmed by sun or exercise. Tesera's large ring bit into his palm.

"I just wish I had known her," he whispered. More than that, he wished she had given him the chance to know her.

"If you recognize her at all, then you know her better than you think, child," said Rose Red.

So many questions bubbled up inside Trix, he felt fit to burst with them, but none seemed worth saying aloud. There were no answers for him here in this tomb. A cloud went over the sun, shrouding the room in strange shadow. From somewhere, Trix could make out the sparkling notes of chimes in the wind. The scent of fading flowers shifted to that of rich earth after a rain.

He looked up to find himself surrounded by a veil of indigo light. Beyond it he could see Rose Red and Lizinia, frozen like statues.

"It's not a bad death, really, for all that it's a rehearsal."

Trix jumped—on the inside, not the out—and turned his head slowly to see the ghost of his mother standing before him. She was the image of the body on the table with her gossamer dress and beflowered hair, only she looked old enough to be one of his own sisters. Another costume. Ever the actress.

"You're not that young anymore," Trix said. "Cut it out."

Tesera hopped spryly off the table and turned a slow circle. When she faced him again she was a wizened old woman. Her clothes and skin both sagged on her frame, but her nose had grown to twice its original size. And had warts. Trix gave her his best look of disappointment.

Tesera burst out laughing. "Oh, you get that from your mother, and no mistake. I'd recognize that face anywhere."

"You *are* my mother." Her laugher annoyed him so much that he took her big blobby nose between his fingers and yanked it off.

Only, it didn't come off. "Ow!" she cried and slapped his hand away. For a frail old bat, she was quite strong. "You don't get it, do you?"

"What, that you may have given birth to me but Mama will always be my mother? Yeah. I get it."

Tesera stiffened, clasped her hands before her, and tilted her head to the side. Even in the old woman's guise it was a perfect imitation of Lizinia. "You are lost in the dark, Trix Woodcutter," she said. "Let me illuminate you."

Her eyes twinkled and the room went black.

"Hello?" Trix's call fell like a thud into the thick darkness. Where was he now? Where was Tesera? Where was anyone?

Trix made out a sparkle in the black. The sparkle grew and became the indigo veil, floating just beyond him like a curtain. There was a figure upon the curtain, a graceful creature he had never seen before…it looked mostly like a large, white deer. The image of it waved as the curtain waved in the nothingness, and Trix moved forward to try and make it out. As he did, the creature split in half like an egg and a giant plume of black smoke rose up from the pieces.

Trix stepped back. He had seen smoke of this like before, when his family had defeated the giant. Aunt Joy had slit the monster's throat and from it had issued what remained of the evil king, a vapor as black and rancid as his soul. That dark cloud had disappeared into the Enchanted Wood. The smoke illustrated here on the curtain continued rising upward and became a dragon, spreading its wings against a star-scattered sky. There was a white, four-legged beast in that sky as well, maybe a tenth the size of the dragon, and on its back were two riders. The dragon sped after the beast and its passengers just as the curtain before him parted.

It seemed that Trix was not to know the outcome of this event, either. Just as well…he wasn't sure if he was supposed to be cheering for the white beast or the dragon.

The stage was set to look like a forest—if not the Enchanted Wood, then a very similar wood all the same. A young man walked carefully through the brush. It was as autumn in the scene as it would be autumn here soon, and the young man did his best to avoid crunching as many of the dried leaves as he could. (Trix could have done better.) He looked about as old as Trix in human years…about as old as Trix now appeared to the rest of the world thanks to Papa Gatto. That rotten, grinning spirit cat…

Trix's wandering thoughts were brought to a halt by a movement in the trees. A movement *of* the trees. It had been so subtle he had almost missed it; in fact, try as he might it was difficult to keep his eyes from losing the anomaly in the foliage. Trix had no firsthand experience with dryads—the people of the trees, the Green Children—but based on tales the animals had told him, Trix gathered that's what he or she was.

"Watch out!" Trix called to the young man as the dryad approached. The young man did not hear him, or pretended not to hear.

In a flash the dryad was upon him from behind, one arm around his neck, one hand over his eyes. The young man yelled and spun around. He grabbed the dryad around the waist, lifted her up and…tickled her? Peals of laugher rang out through the trees. The young man carried the dryad to the stream and quite unceremoniously dropped her in the water.

"Friedrich!" she squealed as the water muddied the paint on her face, arms, and legs. "That's not fair!"

"It's as fair as it is for you to sneak up on me, Ghost." With a smile, Friedrich leaned over the girl in the stream and kissed her soundly. She kissed him back with equal enthusiasm, taking advantage of his precarious state and pulling him down into the water with her.

As the indigo curtains closed over the scene Trix finally recognized the girl.

It was Tesera.

The curtains opened again on a room that looked very similar to the library at the palace in Arilland. A large fireplace lit one end of the room, casting long, dancing shadows across the floor. Friedrich stood in the middle of the room. He had aged since the scene in the woods, but the golden circle on his brow and the thick doublet that he wore made him appear much older.

"I will accept no more excuses from you," Friedrich said to the man before him, with his brown coat worn through in places and his back hunched either by nature or penitence. "Have that gold to me by sundown tomorrow, without exception."

"Yes, sire." The man bowed even lower to Friedrich and politely backed out of the scene. Trix never saw his face.

Friedrich waited a beat in the silence of the room before addressing the emptiness. "I want you to follow him. Make sure he does what I ask."

From a corner of the room that had previously held nothing but shadow, stepped a woman. Her boots, jacket, and trousers were brown and green. All looked to be fashioned from the same supple leather. She wore her cinnamon hair pulled back in a queue. Tesera. Unlike Friedrich, she looked just as young as the girl she had been before...but, like him, her bearing was of someone far older than her years.

"And if he does not?" she asked.

"Then kill him."

The reply did not seem to startle Tesera, who remained in the room with her head bowed.

"You are the only one I can entrust with this task, Ghost," said Friedrich. "You are the only one I trust at all."

"I will do this for you," Tesera said to her boots. "But it will be the last thing you ever ask of me."

Friedrich gave no thought before his reply. "As you wish," he said, and then marched out of the scene in the same direction the sniveling man had departed.

Tesera, now alone in the room, stepped forward. She was but an arm's length from Trix when she stopped and reached behind her back to slide a hidden weapon from its sheath. It was a stiletto, thin and sharp and bright and covered in blood. Tesera's hands were covered in blood now, too.

She looked up—looked Trix dead in the eyes—and dropped the bloody stiletto at his feet as the curtain closed again.

The curtains opened once more onto a forest scene. This was most definitely the Enchanted Wood; Trix knew of no other place in the world where Elder Trees grew as tall and mighty as they did deep in the Wood. A ragwoman sat beside a small campfire, readying a pot of something to set in the embers.

Now that Trix knew what to look for, he began scanning the trees, their trunks, their roots, their leaves, the grass, even the fire itself. Tesera was there somewhere, he knew it, or would be there soon, and he would be ready to spot her. What he was not prepared for was the small rock that randomly tossed itself into the fire. Within seconds the clearing was filled with a sparkly violet fog not unlike the curtain that kept revealing these images to him. When the fog dispersed, there was a knife at the ragwoman's throat. But the attacker was not Tesera.

It was Sorrow.

The evil fairy godmother's ebony hair melted into the darkness around her, but her midnight blue eyes flickered with the flames from the campfire. "It is a rare day indeed that I get the upper hand on you, my slippery, stealthy, sister dearest," Sorrow said in silky tones.

Trix gasped. Tesera had not been hiding from the ragwoman. Tesera *was* the ragwoman.

"What do you want, Sorrow?" Tesera asked in bored tones.

"What do I always want?" Sorrow's grin was even more disturbing than Papa Gatto's. "To make mischief, darling. Same as you."

"I've retired from that life," said Tesera. "I'm naught but an actress now."

"Interesting." Sorrow did not move from behind her sister, nor did she remove the knife from her throat. "I wasn't aware that we could stop being what we are just by deciding it. How marvelous for you."

"You are a pest, Sorrow."

"And you are one of my greatest achievements." Sorrow shifted about, rummaging for something in the pockets of her voluminous cloak. The dagger bit into Tesera's neck, drawing blood and making her wince. Sorrow didn't seem to care. "Drink this." She held out a vial to Tesera with her free hand.

"No, thank you," said Tesera. "I'm afraid you'll just have to kill me."

"Drink it, *Ghost*. Or I will tell him where to find you."

Tesera's body tensed, and then relaxed. She took the vial from Sorrow, pulled the stopper, and drained it.

"NO!" Trix cried futilely. He was baffled. Who was "him?" Friedrich? Trix's birthfather? Trix himself? Someone else entirely? Whoever it was had a powerful enough sway over Tesera to force her to do her chaotic eldest sister's bidding.

Tesera slumped back into Sorrow's arms, unconscious. Sorrow drew a symbol on Tesera's forehead before leaning down to kiss it. The clearing glowed a violet blue again, and then faded.

"Family must stick together," Sorrow whispered to her. "Sweet dreams, my sister." With that, Sorrow shifted into a ragwoman, lifted Tesera's pack, and exited the scene.

Trix tried to run into the Wood to chase Sorrow, to help Tesera, but the stage had already vanished. When he turned back Tesera had reappeared, bedecked once more in white gossamer and flowers.

"Do you understand now?" she asked in a coy voice. *His* voice, when it had been higher pitched and coming from a smaller body.

He understood a lot of things now. Tesera—and no doubt her seamstress sister—was not dead but asleep, under a powerful spell cast by Sorrow. With this spell it seemed that Sorrow had appropriated the sisters' fey gifts as well. Trix also understood that his birthmother's gift was not simply acting, as Aunt Joy had recounted in her stories. Tesera was a glamourist. A chameleon. A ghost.

An assassin.

"Yes," Trix said. "I get it."

"And you do not regret your family?" She honestly sounded like she cared.

He shook his head ever so slightly, his eyes never leaving her translucent form.

"Good," she said. "The Woodcutters were the family you were meant to have. That is how it was meant to be. *You* were meant to be, sweet Trix. You and I....well...we never were. And that will always make me sad, a little. But I will never regret it, as I do not regret the young man standing before me now."

Trix allowed one tear to escape down his cheek.

Tesera slid the large signet ring off her finger and placed it in Trix's hand. "You must take this to the King of the Eagles," she told him. "Will you do that for me?"

It was on the tip of his tongue to tell her that he owed her nothing, but the words dissolved in his brain the moment after he thought them. He could not blame Tesera for being the person she was, nor could he blame her for giving him a family he wouldn't have wanted to grow up without. As much as he wished to be angry, he could not be. However, there was one thing he could do.

He could save her.

"Yes," he said again.

For his acceptance, Tesera gave him a smile that nearly tore his heart in two. "Earth breaks. Fire breathes. Waters bless. Fly away, my son." She reached up, as if to touch him. He felt a cold breeze and the slightest ruffle of hair on the nape of his neck. And then she was gone.

The room did not return right away, nor did the sparkling curtain. Trix took a deep breath into the nothingness and waited.

"DO NOT FEAR, TRIX. I AM WITH YOU."

Trix felt the booming voice deep in his chest. It was a woman's, to be sure, but not his mother's. Before he could ponder it further, the nothingness was gone and the gray sacristy had returned, just as he'd left it.

"If you recognize her at all, then you know her better than you think, child," Rose Red was still in the middle of saying. Now that he fully understood what his aunt meant, he smiled. Trix lifted his hand from his birthmother's. The ring that had previously bit into his fingers now rested loosely in his palm. He clenched the bit of metal in his fist, raising it up to his lips. When he stepped back from the oaken table, he staggered.

Lizinia was by his side in an instant. "Are you all right?"

Trix quickly regained his composure. "I'm fine. I just..." He looked down again at the thick gold and ruby ring in his hand.

"What did she say to you?" asked Rose Red.

Trix gaped at his aunt. "How did you know?"

"There is magic here," Rose Red replied. "I have had visions too, of loved ones passed. A specter came to me last night, as a matter of fact, and informed me of your impending arrival."

"Tesera came to you as well?" he asked.

"It was not my dead sister who spoke to me," said Rose Red. "It was yours."

Trix's heart skipped a beat. Monday's twin Tuesday had danced herself to death in a pair of red shoes not long after his arrival in the

Woodcutter home. He'd been but a babe then. It spoke volumes of her character that Tuesday's shade would still concern herself with her family—never mind her foster brother—even in death.

"But I don't..." As much as Trix would have liked to compare visions and inquire after the possible identity of the goddess who had addressed him at the end of this last one, he decided it was more important to stick to the task at hand. So he started again. "Tesera is not actually dead. She mentioned something about this being a rehearsal, and then I saw... I saw Sorrow. She made Tesera drink a potion, and then she stole her gift."

"*Goddess.*" Rose Red cursed under her breath. "It does explain how she managed to overwhelm our other sister so soon after. It explains a great many things." Rose Red lifted her eyes to the heavens. "And I am afraid of them all." She crossed to the oaken table and adjusted the flowers in Tesera's hair. "Either way, I will keep her body safe from harm. I can promise you that."

"Thank you," said Trix. "But there was something else. She told me to take her ring to the King of Eagles. I hope he'll know why, because I'm sure I don't. Do you?"

He opened his hand to reveal the ring in his outstretched palm. The look his aunt gave him was one of patient benevolence. Trix had seen that same look on his sister Friday's face whenever she delivered bad news.

"My dear nephew," said Rose Red. "The King of Eagles is your father."

10

The Decision of Every Adventurer

he Boy Who Talks to Animals is an age old prophecy," said Rose Red. She had invited Lizinia and Trix back to her rooms for tea and refreshment and further clarification.

Trix was glad for all of those things, but mostly the food. This new body seemed to require far more sustenance than Trix was used to and he was *starving*.

"After Sorrow and Joy turned out to be such forces of nature, it was always thought that my twin would be the one in whose womb that prophecy would be fulfilled. We were the fifth and sixth daughters born to our family," she explained to Lizinia. "Unlike Seven, Trix's foster mother, the rest of us took names instead of numbers as we grew into ourselves. And so my twin and I became

Snow White and Rose Red, after the roses outside our front door."

"Like the roses on the abbey wall," said Lizinia.

The abbess smiled at the golden girl. "Those grew from clippings of the very same bushes."

The red velvet cushion of the abbess's guest chair was thin and lumpy. Trix didn't relish the thought of sitting here all afternoon chatting about flowers. "The lingworm said that I was 'a story told before the gods were gods,' and that I was meant to be a voice for all the animals. When were the gods not gods?"

Rose Red closed her eyes and shook her head. "Of course you met the lingworm."

Before his aunt could answer his question, Lizinia asked another one. "If this prophecy has been around for so long, why hasn't it come to fruition before now?" She sat perfectly still, the picture of ease and contentment. Trix was convinced that the layer of gold on her skin and clothes made Lizinia impervious to discomfort.

"This has been the issue of much theological debate," answered Rose Red. "A boy who could communicate with every animal on earth would need powers beyond that of the ancient Animal Kings."

Trix agreed. There were three kinds of animals in the world: regular animals, humans who had been cursed into taking animal form, and magical animals with the enchanted blood of the Animal Kings. It was said that this last group had the power to change form under the light of the full moon. To the best of Trix's knowledge, he had never met one of the enchanted beasts in human form, but the Animal Kings certainly knew of his existence.

"So the prophetic progeny would need to be one half Animal King, and one half...god?" asked Lizinia.

"Or fey," said Trix. "There are some fey powerful enough to be gods." His aunts were two of them. His sister Wednesday was a third.

"Snow White and I befriended a bear when we were young," Rose Red said to Trix. "Did your Papa ever tell you that tale?"

"No," said Trix. Aunt Joy had revealed their family's true magical nature to the Woodcutter siblings only that spring. What with the killing of the giant and Sunday becoming Queen and all, there hadn't been time for Papa to tell many tales.

"That is a shame. You'll have to ask him sometime. I can't do it justice, for all that it happened to me. Suffice it to say that my sister and I saved the bear from a wretched little man. Mother allowed him to stay with us. Upon the full moon, he revealed that he was the son of the King of Bears, and he asked Snow White to marry him."

"Weren't you jealous?" asked Lizinia. "I know a thing or two about jealous sisters."

"Not in the slightest," said Rose Red. "I loved Bear, truly, but I have never been as romantic as my sister."

"So a Bear Prince married one of the most powerful fey daughters that has ever lived," said Trix.

"It was the perfect match," said Rose Red. "Unfortunately, Snow White is barren."

Lizinia gave a small gasp. "Oh! How sad."

"I agree," said the abbess. "They would have had many happy

children together, raised them all in a household where they knew they were loved."

"As I was," murmured Trix.

"As you were meant to," said Rose Red. "The stars had aligned. Our world shook with chaos. It was time for the Boy Who Talks to Animals to be born. And since Snow White and Bear could not have that child, the gods arranged a dalliance between your birthmother and the King of Eagles."

A brown-robed monk finally appeared with a tray of tea that smelled of jasmine and raspberries and a pile of cakes, which Trix immediately fell upon and devoured. "So what happened between Tesera and the King of Eagles?" he asked between bites.

"You'll have to ask him," was all Rose Red supplied before she sipped her tea.

"Do you know where we can find him?"

"Farther to the north and east, for his is one of the Lands of Immortality. Beyond that, I cannot tell you."

Trix contemplated the small weight of Wisdom's tooth, still hung around his neck. "My animal friends will help. I'm sure we can manage."

Slowly, Lizinia's head turned to him and her amber eyes met his. "We?" she asked.

Trix froze with a third cake halfway to his mouth. He had forgotten the deal that they'd made. Lizinia had offered to accompany him to his mother's grave, and she had done that. As much as he would have loved her company on this next leg of his journey, the image of her golden form smothered in black wasps niggled at the back of his mind. Yes, she could hold her own in a fight well enough, and he could learn to deal with her smarmy feline godfather. But even in this new body, he didn't want to be the one responsible for her getting hurt. To whatever extent Lizinia *could* be hurt.

"The abbey does seem to be lovely this time of year," he said. "There are tons of people here you could meet and make friends with. You could probably do any job you want here, and I bet they wouldn't ever make you eat apples again if you didn't want to. In time you could settle down in a new home, in a new place, though I'm sure Rose Red wouldn't mind if you stayed." He didn't sound quite as convincing as he wanted to. Trix looked to his aunt for help, but Rose Red suddenly seemed very interested in her tea.

Lizinia tilted her head in that very Lizinia way of hers. Trix would miss that about her. "Don't you want me to come with you?" she asked plainly.

"Of course I do," said Trix. "But I cannot promise you safe passage and easy roads."

"We took no safe passages or easy roads to get here, Trix Woodcutter. But we arrived all the same."

"We did," he said. "But I'm not... My family is not like normal families."

"As I have seen."

"Then you can believe me when I say that my life is not a normal life. Chaos follows me around, Lizinia. I suspect your godfather knew that, or he wouldn't have done *this* to me. You may choose to travel with me at your peril."

"The decision of every adventurer," Rose Red said from inside her teacup, "is whether or not it's worth the risk. This is the most important decision."

"So, what do you think?" Trix asked his golden girl. "Am I worth the risk?"

"Yes," Lizinia said with a smile. And because her answer made him incredibly happy, Trix smiled back.

"Then I will ready supplies for your journey without delay," Rose Red said, and left the room.

"I'm going to walk the gardens one more time before we leave if that's all right," said Lizinia.

"That's fine," he said. "I'll come collect you when everything's ready. In the meantime, I'm going to hunt down some more of those cakes."

Lizinia turned down the corridor that led to the courtyard, while Trix made his way down the winding hallways of the great abbey in an attempt to find either the kitchens or the monk who'd brought the tea tray. He disturbed room after room of acolytes at study and dedicates in prayer and Sisters in their private chambers. Finally, Trix found the monk, just inside the grand mahogany doors of Rose Abbey's entranceway.

The hood of the Brother's brown robes was pulled down over his face, but Trix recognized him because of his size—few people were both as tall as Saturday and as broad shouldered as Papa. Miraculously, the tray he carried was once again filled with cakes. Trix sent up a prayer to the Earth Goddess. This was her place, after all, and it very well might have been she who had addressed him in his vision.

"Excuse me, Brother!" Trix called out as he caught up with the monk. "Would it be possible to get my hands on a few more of those tasty cakes?"

The monk stopped his forward progress and chuckled low as he turned around. He set the tray of cakes down on the seat of a bench in the hall. "Of course, little brother. Help yourself."

Trix did indeed, stuffing cakes into his mouth and pockets at the same time. The delicate desserts melted on his tongue. Some were buttery and filled with berries; some were heavier and thick with spice. All of them were creamy and fluffy and delicious. It might have been his fey blood that craved the sweetness. If he could eat cakes every day of his life, he would die a happy boy. Man. Prince. Whatever.

"I suppose they won't have those where you're going?" Trix could tell the Brother was smiling.

As Trix chewed in blissful delight, he considered the carnivorous carrion diet of eagles. Cakes were definitely not on the menu. "No sir," he said to the Brother. "I plan to enjoy them while I can."

"Good man," said the monk.

"Why do you wear your hood so low?" It was a good thing Mama wasn't around to scold Trix for asking impertinent questions of strangers or talking with his mouth full.

"I have taken a vow of humility," said the monk.

Trix swallowed the berry cake. The Brother was lying. He wasn't sure why a monk would lie, but Trix had enough experience stretching the truth to recognize it in others. Before he could ask about that, too, there was a pounding knock on the enormous entranceway doors. The monk did not move to answer the summons. Instead, he stomped on the ground beneath the table, took Trix by the neck of his shirt, and shoved him into a tapestry across the hallway. But Trix did not slam into the wall; he fell through the secret door that had been opened by the catch on the floor. Quickly, the monk ducked under the tapestry as well.

The secret room was dark with shadow, but light shone through the tapestry here and there, revealing gaps in the weave. Fascinated, Trix picked himself up off the flagstones. He stepped up to the tapestry and peered through one of larger holes. He could still see the entranceway and the table and the tray of cakes.

The knock stopped, and then started again with renewed vigor. "Shouldn't someone see to that?" whispered Trix. "It sounds...important."

"It is not for you," the Brother whispered back. He, too, peered through a gap higher up in the design's weave. Why the secrecy? Was the abbey being invaded? Had the evil Sorrow sent an army of goblins to attack them? Had the wasps hunted him down? Trix convinced himself that each of these things were possible, and yet in none of the scenarios did it make sense for the enemy to knock on the front door.

After several more rounds of pounding, Rose Red appeared. She straightened her robes, and then gave the order for the guards to pull the doors open. The abbess obviously suspected the identity of the impatient visitor. She was just as obviously surprised to discover their true identity.

"Thursday!" she cried.

Trix was as shocked as his aunt. "Thursday?"

The monk held him back, placing an enormous hand over his mouth. "Shh. Wait."

Annoyed, Trix nodded and the Brother lowered his hand. They watched as a lithe woman with a riot of red curls burst over the threshold to embrace the abbess. Trix gaped. Thursday had run away to sea when he was but a child. In all the years she'd been gone, he had half expected the Pirate Queen to have become a giantess like Saturday. Compared to their warrior sister, Thursday was *petite*.

Behind her, several men carried a stretcher that bore... He strained to see through the tapestry, but Trix could not make out if it was a man or a woman.

Rose Red stepped forward and examined the body herself. She raised her eyes to the ceiling, as she did when praying to the goddess. Then she sighed and shook her head. "Oh, Seven."

This time, Trix's hand rose to cover his own mouth. The body the men carried was Mama Woodcutter.

Sorrow had struck again.

"She fell asleep and I couldn't wake her," said Thursday. "I would say she's sick, but there are no symptoms. I can't even make out a heartbeat."

"But you know she's not dead." It was a statement more than a question, but well enough asked; Rose Red herself had not recognized this same sleeping spell on her other sisters.

"I know," said Thursday. "I have seen enough dead men to know."

"Take her to the chapel," Rose Red said to the men. And then to Thursday, "Do not worry, child. All will be well. Now, come in. Rest yourself. And then tell me what happened." The abbess put an arm around the Pirate Queen and led her down the hallway in the opposite direction from the room behind the tapestry.

Thursday was here. Trix gave the knowledge a moment to sink in. He couldn't wait to talk with her. She might have some idea of what to do about Sorrow. Thursday always did seem to know a little bit about everything. Now that Mama had been struck down as well, something definitely needed to be done. Whatever Sorrow's plans, her actions were escalating. With the stolen gifts of three sisters under her belt, who knew how powerful she was now? She had to be stopped. This business with the King of Eagles could wait…though he suspected Tesera would haunt him mercilessly until he completed his task.

"It seems that the abbess will be too busy to tend to your supplies," the monk said softly. His hands were clenched into fists at his sides. "I'll see to your packs myself so you can be on your way."

Trix was no longer concerned with remaining undiscovered. "*On my way?* My renegade sister just showed up with the cursed body of my mother and I'm supposed to turn my back on them for a fool's errand?"

"You know for sure she's cursed?" asked the monk.

"Okay, not really a curse, but it's hard to explain."

"Try."

"See, I have this evil aunt. For whatever reason, it seems she is stealing the powers of her sisters to use for her own devices. That"—Trix pointed in the direction of the entranceway—"was my mother, and Mama's gift is really powerful, so we're all in pretty big trouble and *I need to help now*."

Trix tried to dodge past the monk and escape from the secret room as he finished the rambling elucidation, but the Brother caught him. Trix fought with his new body and his new strength— he was a far more formidable foe than he'd ever been. Even still, the bigger and stronger Brother got the best of him in the end. The monk forced Trix's hands to his sides, but not before Trix threw out an elbow and knocked back his hood.

For a moment, they both froze.

"Ja—?"

There was a hand over Trix's mouth again before the word could fully escape. The smattering of light through the tapestry holes revealed dark blond hair and ice blue eyes. He was the spitting image of Papa and Saturday in form *and* face...this could be no other than Jack Woodcutter. Myth. Legend. Eldest of the Woodcutter siblings and supposedly long since dead and gone.

This *was* a day for surprises.

Jack lowered his hand. Trix stared at his brother in silence. He grinned a little, despite the grim circumstances in which he found himself. "Sunday was right."

Jack's half-smile mirrored his own. "I look forward to meeting her. Someday."

"Someday?" asked Trix. "But why not now? If you're here, and you're alive, and you know where we are, then why don't you come home? You can't abandon us again now. You have to help us find a way to help Mama."

"I just…it's…" Jack closed his eyes and pursed his lips in thought. "Auntie Rose was wrong," he said finally, seemingly apropos of nothing.

Luckily, context had never been a problem for Trix. Important things usually revealed themselves sooner or later. "Wrong about what?" he asked.

"The decision of every adventurer," said Jack. "The most important one is not based on risk. Every adventurer accepts risk. That's what makes us adventurous to begin with."

Trix might not have believed this coming from anyone else, but if there was a body who knew about adventures, it was Jack Woodcutter. "Then what is it?"

"The most important decision of every adventurer is which path to take, and which to leave behind."

Of course, Jack was right. Trix hated him a little for that.

Five minutes ago, he'd had plans for his future. If he was going to throw those plans out the window, he owed it to himself—to Lizinia—to be sure. Trix's mind raced. He could stay here and help his sister and brother, or he could leave Thursday and Jack in Rose Red's care and set out on Tesera's quest. Perhaps, on their travels, Trix and Lizinia might even find the cure for Sorrow's sleeping spell. Trix did have a tendency to be lucky in that way. Stranger things had happened.

"I need to find Lizinia," said Trix. "We have to go."

Jack nodded. "I'll have packs waiting for you here in the entranceway. Do you know which direction to travel?"

Trix recalled what Rose Red had told them in her sitting room. "North and east, to the Lands of Immortality."

Jack clapped Trix on the shoulder. "Good man."

"Thank you." And because he wasn't sure when he would ever again have the chance, Trix threw himself into his brother's arms. "I love you, Jack. We all love you. Please stay alive."

Jack's strong arms squeezed him as tightly as Papa's. "You too, little brother. You too."

As soon as Trix broke away from the embrace he hit the door at a run, leaving his legendary brother and his cakes far behind. He kept on running, until he found Lizinia in the gardens.

"Come on, Goldilocks!" Trix called. "It's time to go!"

Lizinia had either forgotten her previous stance on nicknames or forgiven him immediately, for she shot back with, "Right behind you, Scapegrace."

"Good one," he said.

"I asked the acolytes," she admitted.

"Cheater!" Her eyes widened at that, and he took her hand. "But I forgive you. We have plenty of time to think up more on the road."

She squeezed his fingers with her own. "Then let's get to it, shall we? Adventure awaits!"

ACKNOWLEDGEMENTS

Trix's adventures started back in 2012—the fall after *Enchanted*'s release. I had just turned in the first draft of *Hero* and was playing around with *Trixter* in the "free time" I had while I awaited that first painful round of revisions. Per my editor's request, the character of Trix had been almost completely written out of the novel. Not a small feat, when one considers that the whole impetus for Saturday's journey was chasing after Trix when he ran away from home...

I had an inkling of all the trouble Trix got himself into while Saturday was imprisoned in the White Mountains, but how was I supposed to tell that story? The Woodcutter Sisters books were meant to be just that: one book about each *sister*, leaving no room for Trix.

But...we love Trix!

In 2014, two fortuitous things happened: Harcourt decided not to extend a contract for more Woodcutter Sisters books, and my best friend Casey read that partial draft of *Trixter*.

The moment the publisher declined our pitch for books 4-7, I was released from my "option clause," meaning that I now had the freedom to do whatever I wanted with the series (including MAKING THE ACKNOWLEDGEMENTS AS LONG AS I WANT). This is the point where most writers would give up on a world they've spent a lifetime creating and move onto other things.

Luckily for Woodcutter fans, I am not like most writers.

I have eaten, slept, and breathed fairy tales since I was a small child. I may have secured a bachelor's degree in science, but I never strayed from my folklorish roots. Authors are told to write what we know. What I know are fairy tales.

Which brings us to Casey, my best friend from seventh grade and my very first writing partner. We composed epic fantasy novels together, and poetry, and many short stories about princesses. I went on to make a career out of princess stories. Casey went on to become Associate Professor of English at Winthrop University. One of her most popular classes? Fairy tales and folklore. *Enchanted* is required reading.

So I sent *Trixter* to Casey, this half-draft sort-of idea for a (story? novella? novel?) about Trix. She got back to me with detailed comments. Apparently, what I'd thought was the first half of a story was really a beginning and end with no middle. Trix had to *suffer*. There had to be *obstacles*, and those obstacles needed to be overcome. A phone call transpired, involving a certain amount of enthusiastic brainstorming.

I will always remember that moment of Grand Epiphany when I realized Casey should be My Editor. (The clouds parted and angels sang and everything!) It just made so much *sense*, and you know how I feel about things making sense.

And so my first acknowledgement must go out to my beloved Casey Cothran, without whom Trix might never have had an adventure at all.

Huge thanks as well to my dear parents—the real Mama and Papa Woodcutter—Marcy and George Kontis, without whom I might never have survived the escape of a bad situation and the rebuilding of the beautiful life I have now in Florida. This princess loves you to the edge of the Milky Way and beyond!

I would also like to thank the rest of the team who worked to put this book in your hot little hands: my phenomenally talented cover artist Rachel Marks and my new best friend, copyeditor Kat Tipton. Gratitude must be extended as well to my advisors and mentors during this transition: J. T. Ellison, Mary B. Rodgers, Anthea Sharp, Leanna Renee Hieber, Stephen Segal, Jude Deveraux, and Roxanne St. Claire.

I must throw buckets of love and glitter to my street team, otherwise known as Princess Alethea's Brute Squad. Never would I have imagined that such a magical community of smart, helpful, fun, and funny people would be brought together because of something I created. From proofreading and cover copy creation to making memes and assisting on book tour, these folks have done EVERYTHING...up to and including a neverending supply of virtual hugs and constantly picking me up when I'm feeling low.

Princess Alethea's Brute Squad: Courtney Ballard, Paula and Mark Beauchamp, Dee Bitner, Samantha Bitner, Tracy Blackwell, John and Michelle Bowen, Ann Bridges, Rebekah Brown, Shondra Bush, Laura Carrubba, Krystn Cedzidlo, Margaret Coin, Jean-Louis Couturier, Kat Crouch, Krys Doty, Jacquelyne Drainville, Bethany Dunlap, Sarah Elmore, Ben English, Christa Ermer, Mindy Evans, Amy French, Danielle Greer, Ashley Gustafson, Melinda Hamby, Sarah Harvey, Beth Henkel, Cherokee Hensley, Annie Jackson, Lillie James, Carolina Johnson, Jennifer Kelley, Linwood Knight, Bev Kodak, Nessa Kreyling, Liz

Mangold, Jeanne Martin, Robin McClure, Kitti McConnell, Fredrica Mitchell, Todd Muldrew, Matina Newsome, Jenney O'Callaghan, Mandy Poitras, Aaron and Angela Pound, Michelle Ristuccia, Bronwyn Roos, Shannan Rosa, Melissa Royer, Marie Sherman, Christina Shirley, Dee Sixx, Crystal Smalling, Megan Stone, Dee Sunday, Jacque Sue-Ping, Amanda Thompson, Bonnie Wagner, and Leighanna Walsh.

Last but not least, a million thanks to my Fairy Godagent Deborah Warren, for believing in me and sticking by my side when I propose six impossible things before breakfast…and then proceeded to accomplish every single one.

I love you all like family. But I suspect you already know that.

ABOUT THE AUTHOR

New York Times and USA Today bestselling author Alethea Kontis is a princess, a fairy godmother, and a geek. She's known for screwing up the alphabet, scolding vampire hunters, and ranting about fairy tales on YouTube.

Her published works include: *The Wonderland Alphabet* (with Janet K. Lee), *Diary of a Mad Scientist Garden Gnome* (with Janet K. Lee), the AlphaOops series (with Bob Kolar), the Books of Arilland fairy tale series, and *The Dark-Hunter Companion* (with Sherrilyn Kenyon). Her short fiction, essays, and poetry have appeared in a myriad of anthologies and magazines.

Alethea's debut YA fairy tale novel *Enchanted* won the Gelett Burgess Children's Book Award in 2012 and the Garden State Teen Book Award in 2015. *Enchanted* was nominated for the Audie Award in 2013, and was selected for World Book Night in 2014. Both *Enchanted* and its sequel, *Hero*, were nominated for the Andre Norton Award.

Born in Burlington, Vermont, Alethea currently lives and writes on the Space Coast of Florida. She makes the best baklava you've ever tasted and sleeps with a teddy bear named Charlie. You can find Princess Alethea on all the social media and her website: www.aletheakontis.com.